THE HOMELESS HERO

a novel

LEE SILBER

ALSO BY LEE SILBER

A Parent Looks at Fifty

Runaway Best Seller

Summer Stories

Show And Tell Organizing

No Brown M&Ms

The Ripple Effect

Creative Careers

Bored Games

The Wild Idea Club

Rock To Riches

Chicken Soup For The Beach Lover's Soul (Contributor)

Organizing From The Right Side Of The Brain

Money Management For The Creative Person

Self-Promotion For The Creative Person

Career Management For The Creative Person

Time Management For The Creative Person

Aim First

Notes, Quotes & Advice

Successful San Diegans

Dating in San Diego

THE HOMELESS HERO

a novel

LEE SILBER

THE HOMELESS HERO

Lee Silber

Published by Deep Impact Publishing
822 Redondo Court
San Diego CA 92109

To buy copies of this book in bulk, inquire about a presentation based on this story, or get a free copy of the companion guide featuring photographs of the places featured in the book, please contact the author at:

www.leesilber.com, 858-735-4533, leesilber@leesilber.com

Cover and Interior Design: Lee Silber
Layout and Typesetting: Social Motion Publishing

First Print Edition January 2015

This is a work of fiction. All the names, characters, and places are either invented or used fictitiously. The exception is the fact that eight players from the 1984 San Diego Chargers football team are in fact now dead..

Retail Price: $11.00

To all those who have faced adversity and risen above it.

"They say football is a matter of life and death—but it's more important than that."

—BILL SHANKLY

CHAPTER 1

A FEW FEET BELOW THE SURFACE, THOMAS MacDonald remained perfectly still. His only means of survival, several Starbucks straws linked together and protruding an inch above the ground, providing him just enough oxygen to breathe through the layer of dirt concealing his location. For Thomas, the hardest part about being buried alive was remembering to breathe through his mouth and not his nose. He also had to fight to keep his eyes clenched shut. He fought the urge to inhale through his nostrils and open his eyes, but his instincts and over forty years of habit made it hard to resist. He knew if he did his lungs would instantly fill with dirt and he would start thrashing around and give away his position. He couldn't afford to be caught. Instead he stayed perfectly still, listening to the sound of air going in and out of his makeshift breathing tube and the faint voices of the police searching the surrounding area.

He squirmed as a bug began crawling up his pants leg. He wanted to scream, but instead he clenched his eyes shut and slowed his breathing down to next to nothing to keep from panicking. When the rather large insect reached his knee, Thomas carefully moved his hand over and pressed down on his pants. He felt the bug squish but it continued to squirm, so he pressed harder to make sure it was dead.

Besides the lack of oxygen and the bugs, being buried alive had its advantages—it had a way of clearing the mind of trivial things and allowed Thomas to think back to how he ended up in this prickly predicament.

If someone had told him a few years ago he would be broke and homeless and hiding from the cops, he would have laughed in their face. At that time he was on top of the world. He'd just retired from playing pro football for the Chargers, his hometown team. As an offensive lineman, he wasn't a household name, but to the people who knew the game (and mattered to him), he was considered one of the best at what he did.

He met and married the girl of his dreams (or so he thought) and they had two beautiful children. Unlike a lot of other players, his transition from a lengthy career in the NFL to "the real world" was smooth. He pursued his other passion—building things—and his construction company thrived. He spent his spare time designing and building his dream home in the Bird Rock area of La Jolla—doing much of the work himself. He was as happy as he'd ever been—considering he was suffering the side effects of playing organized football since he was ten years old.

The repeated blows to his head year after year as a lineman were like being in an endless series of serious car crashes. The reasons for his early retirement from football were the horrible headaches, insomnia, and wild mood swings that had gotten progressively worse. The fact that these symptoms continued even after he stopped playing football was frustrating, but he was used to "playing through pain" and he soldiered on with the help of pills and booze. It was his futile efforts to self-medicate the pain away that proved to be a pivotal turning point in his life and the beginning of the end. If he could have just reached out for assistance, maybe this wouldn't have happened to him. But he was too proud to admit he had a problem and needed help (like two of his former teammates who took their own lives), and that was his undoing. He knew that tonight, but if the cops found him here now, he would lose everything... again.

CHAPTER 2

THOMAS SLOWED HIS BREATHING WAY DOWN and started counting his breaths as a way to focus on inhaling through his mouth—and keep track of time. He figured the police would give up their halfhearted search for him in a few minutes and then post a patrol car curbside after that. He would need to remain buried for at least another 30 minutes before he could crawl out of his hole and make his escape—as he had done a dozen times before.

After the divorce, the courts ruled he could no longer visit his own children—or even be in the same zip code. So, the desperate dad dug a hidey-hole little by little at night so he would have a place to squirrel away if he was ever discovered watching his kids through the window of the custom one-story ranch home he'd built for his family. The hole was partially hidden by shrubs on one side and a large planter box below the living room window—the window where he had to hide and watch his son grow up before his eyes, but without him.

He inhaled again, but this time no air came through the extended straw—so he sucked in harder. Nothing. Having his air supply cut off was not part of the plan. He tried again, and again no air came in. He attempted to breathe out, but the straw was clogged. He didn't want to panic, but being trapped under a layer of dirt with no oxygen had a way of making one freak out. He had no choice; he had to surface.

As he started to lose consciousness, Thomas began clawing his way out of the damp and dark hole he was in, but there was something on his chest holding him down. Even though he'd contemplated suicide several times, he knew he would never be able to go through with it when his will to live (and be there for his children) kicked in. As a former NFL offensive lineman, he was both big and strong and he used old familiar muscles to move the obstacle on his chest off and to the side. He burst through the dirt and filled his lungs with air—but what he saw took his breath away.

Laying on her side was Abby, his twelve-year-old daughter. Thomas quickly leapt to his feet and turned over his little girl, ready to revive her. Then he saw it, her mouth curled into a small grin. Her eyes were closed, but she was faking it.

"You. It was you? Abby!" Thomas yelled a little too loudly.

"Shhhhhh. Sorry, dad. But you should have seen your face when you pushed me off and popped up. At least I know you care," she whispered.

"Of course I care. Why do you think I'm here?"

"I don't know, dad, why *are* you here?" Abby said as she sat up.

"It's the only time I get to see your brother."

"I know, Dad. I know," Abby said with sadness in her voice.

"Who called the police? Your mother or your *new* father?" Thomas wanted to know.

"It was mom. She was really mad when Alex said he saw you looking in the window. She said..."

"I'm sure you shouldn't repeat what your mom said about me, young lady. Your brother saw me and then told your mom where I was. Really?"

"Give him time, dad. He'll come around," Abby said, sounding much wiser than her dozen years.

"I hope so, Abby. It's so hard not spending time with him. I miss him so much."

"He misses you, too. He just won't admit it," Abby said, now standing, in the hedges next to the house she was raised in. The big man was 6-foot-5, but he was a sensitive guy who wasn't afraid to show his emotions. His daughter knew this, having seen him cry on more than one occasion. When he first found out her mom was leaving him and insisted he move out, he cried. When the judge told him he could no longer visit his kids, he cried. When he found out his ex-wife's boyfriend moved in, he cried. Pretty much every time his daughter snuck out to see him he had tears in his eyes. She hugged him tight, clearly not caring that her father was caked in dirt.

"What time is it?" Thomas asked.

Abby pulled her iPhone out of her back pocket. Like many kids her age, she never went anywhere without it, even to bed. As the time popped up on the screen, she cupped the phone with her hand to hide the light of the display. "It's a little after ten. Why?"

"You should be in bed. But first tell me if you saw

any police around."

"No. I wouldn't have done this if they were still here. They drove off right before I came out."

"Alright then. Well, get yourself to bed now." She nodded, but remained, hesitating for a moment. He knew she had something to say. "Yeah, Abby?"

"I'll see you tomorrow after school." In the faint light of a nearby streetlamp, he could see her smile, and he smiled back.

Thomas knew it was a violation of the restraining order against him for Abby to spend time with him in the camper van he called home—but he also didn't try to stop her from coming, either. How could he? He loved having her around, and they both loved Mariner's Beach Park where he often hung out. Despite all that happened, their relationship was solid. Plus, she was a really smart kid and he enjoyed their long talks about everything from sports to politics. Thankfully, she wasn't interested in boys and seemed completely unaware at how quickly she was developing into a young woman. She wore her long blonde hair pulled back in a ponytail, preferred comfortable clothes to the more revealing things her classmates tended to wear, and had hazel eyes that were striking even without makeup. She knew the crazy cast of characters who called the beach park home and they all knew her, and a couple even helped her with her homework—under Thomas's supervision—so that's where she spent many an afternoon.

"Don't you have friends from school you want to hang out with instead of a beaten-down old man?"

"Dad, you're not old! Okay, you're kinda old. But you aren't beaten down. You're as strong as anyone I know. However, we could say you *are* a dirty old man," Abby said with a smile, nodding at the dirt in her father's long stringy hair, bushy beard, and filthy clothes.

"Very funny," Thomas said as he brushed off some of the caked-in dirt. But it would take a long hot shower to really get clean—something he didn't have access to. A cold shower, yes. A hot shower, not a chance. He'd built a makeshift shower with a small enclosure next to his van using parts he'd found laying around, but he rarely used it because he didn't want the entire homeless population to come over to strip down and clean up. Usually Thomas would just jump in the ocean to clean off as best he could. That was simple to do since he lived at the beach... like a lot of homeless people. They just didn't have beach *houses*. The spot he chose to park his van and create his little slice of heaven was located in the far corner of the camp on a prime piece of property within proximity of both the beach and Mission Bay. The camp was in an old abandoned RV park the homeless sought refuge in a few years earlier. How long they would be able to stay there was anyone's guess, but at least Thomas had a place he could call home for the moment, which was an upgrade from when he hit rock bottom and slept *on* the beach instead of near it.

"Dad, on those rare occasions when you clean yourself up, you don't look half bad. You cut your hair, trim your beard, and get some new clothes and maybe mom will take you back."

"I don't think so, Abby. It's not..."

She cut him off with a wave of her hand and said, "I'll see you at three o'clock tomorrow, okay? Good night, Dad," she said as she stretched her lanky frame to kiss him on the cheek. Thomas was reluctant to turn and walk away from everything that meant anything to him, but it was a long walk back to the camp.

"Good night, sweetheart," the big man said with tears in his eyes as he watched his little girl climb back into her bedroom through her window—she had long ago figured out how to bypass the alarm. He smiled with pride. She was a good girl with just a touch of mischief in her. Little did he know he'd soon find out how clever his daughter really was.

CHAPTER 3

THE NEXT MORNING, THOMAS UNLOCKED THE side door to his customized yellow VW camper van and quickly slid it open so he could get a glimpse of the sunrise. That's when he heard the scream.

"Yowzah! Hot, hot, hot," Shaggy said as he brushed the spilled coffee off his ratty surplus Army jacket. "Damn, Big Mac, that was my good jacket."

"Shaggy, that's your only jacket, and you know it," Thomas said to his filthy friend, whose real name few people knew. In fact, those who called the trailer park home all went by nicknames since many were running from something—or someone. Thomas MacDonald wasn't running from anyone. He'd been called "Big Mac" since his first day at training camp with the San Diego Chargers. It was a combination of his last name being MacDonald, his enormous size—and a little hazing by the veterans. The older players made the rookie drive to McDonald's and purchase enough Big Macs to feed the entire team. The bill came close to $300, but he didn't really care since he was a first-round draft pick who had just signed a big contract. That was then, this was now. The people around him still called him Big Mac, but the people around him were homeless—just like him.

"What'd you do, dig a ditch and sleep in the dirt last night? You're filthy," Shaggy said.

"You're one to talk," Thomas replied, ignoring Shaggy's insightful comment as he waved for his friend to join him in his van. This wasn't any ordinary van. It was the first thing Thomas had bought with his signing bonus back in 1983, and it was beautiful. The custom-built 1970 VW "pop top" camper van came complete with a couch, tiny kitchen (with a small sink and a mini-fridge), a booth with a table for two, and other amenities. Using his carpentry skills, Thomas made even more improvements and innovative storage solutions to his pride and joy. He parked it in the mini-compound he built at the park using his skills as a former home-builder. Tapping into the power and water was a lot easier since the plumbing and electrical connections were still there from the glory days of the park when families came with their RVs for summer vacations. Now, not so much.

Shaggy slipped into the booth while Thomas made them a pot of coffee, throwing away his now-empty cup. "Yeah, well I don't live in the lap of luxury like you do," Shaggy said. "Try sleeping out in the cold for a week or two and see how clean you look."

"What happened to your car?" Thomas asked.

"Don't ask."

"I already did," Thomas said while "cleaning" a coffee cup by wiping it with his shirt.

"Consider it asked and answered then."

The truth was Shaggy got his nickname because of the way he dressed. Like a lot of homeless people he layered his clothes since his body also served as his closet. His choice of apparel tended to be ragged and large, and because he was so lanky (and probably more than a little malnourished), everything kind of hung off him—he looked a lot like Shaggy (albeit an African-American version) from the *Scooby Doo* cartoons, with his curly and unruly head of hair and scraggly goatee.

The two were close friends, which was not the norm with people who were virtually homeless. Since most were in a constant state of desperation, they did what they had to do to survive—which often meant sticking it to your "friends" to get the next fix or food to eat. Shaggy didn't use drugs, and Thomas had gotten a handle on his pain pill problem. (The problem was he couldn't afford them, and the solution was to ration what little he had left.) Drinking a little too much was another story, however, and any conflict they'd had in the past was the result of being over-served... by themselves. When Thomas presented Shaggy with his fresh cup of coffee, Shaggy took a sip and then added in some rum from a flask. For Shaggy, happy hour lasted all day and well into the night.

"B.M., did you—" Shaggy started to say.

"I told you, don't call me that. It makes it sound like my nickname is short for a bowel movement. Call me Thomas, T.M., or Big Mac, alright?"

Shaggy knew better than to anger the big man. Even though he was a gentle giant, Shaggy had seen him use his crazy-good martial arts moves more than once to beat the crap out of anyone who thought they could steal his stuff. Shaggy later learned that Thomas had studied Aikido as a way to win the hand-to-hand combat every offensive lineman engages in with defenders attempting to get to the quarterback he was tasked to protect. Big Mac told him it was the same kind of karate moves Steven Seagal used in his movies, and like the actor, Thomas had fallen in love with the discipline and went on to become a black belt and master of martial arts.

"No problem, T-h-o-m-a-s. I was wondering, have you seen Teen Wolf? He's been MIA since last week."

"Come to think of it, I haven't seen him around. The last time I talked to Mike was about a week ago, I think. I asked him about convincing the judge to give me visitation rights with my kids. He said he would look into it and get back to me this week."

"His real name is Mike?"

"Yeah, I knew him before he lost his license to practice law. He kinda borrowed money from his clients and then gambled it away."

"Ah, so gambling is his issue."

"Among other things. He was a really good attorney before he went to the dark side, so I asked him to look into my case. Whether he can get into the law library looking like he does is another story."

"How old do you think he is?" Shaggy asked, taking a sip of his booze-filled brew.

"He's gotta be in his late fifties by now, but he looks like he's a kid, which is how he got Teen Wolf as his street name."

"Plus the big bushy beard he's always sported."

"Exactly. Let's go take a walk over to his spot and see if he's around. I was kinda counting on him to come through for me. Not being able to see my son is killing me. Shaggy, let me put your coffee in a go-cup and top it off, you can put a little of that rum in mine."

The two friends walked from Big Mac's prime corner spot overlooking the bay to where Teen Wolf had his makeshift shack at the other end of the park. Just like in the real world, homeless people could achieve social status based on what they had and where they lived. Thomas was considered wealthy since he slept in his van and had built a custom compound in his desirable and cozy corner lot of the camp. In addition to a storage shed and an outhouse, Thomas had constructed a porch with an awning, all made from scrap wood. It wasn't pretty, but it was pretty cool to have a place to store his stuff, get out of the sun, not to mention go to the bathroom in private.

Thomas, like everyone else here, was a squatter and city officials could come in and level their compound if they wanted to—but that would be a public relations disaster so they looked the other way as the homeless turned the former trailer park into a quasi refugee camp. At one time, this had been a beautiful place with mobile homes, campers, and campsites all on perfectly groomed grounds with security and a property management office. While the rights to the land languished in the courts, the homeless moved in and took over the "upkeep" and "management" of the prime property... security was another matter.

As they approached Teen Wolf's space, the first thing they noticed was his old beaten-up green backpack propped up next to a porta-potty he'd somehow acquired. On the side of the porta-potty it read in big bold letters, "Property of Johnny-on-the-Spot Rentals" (but they were no longer servicing it, based on the smell).

"You see what I see, Shaggy?"

"A place to take a leak in private?"

"No, his backpack is still here. He never goes anywhere without his old Army surplus bag flung over his shoulder. I hope he isn't another one of us to vanish into thin air."

"This would make, what, six in the past two months?" Shaggy wondered aloud.

"More than that. I know of at least a dozen people from this camp who have disappeared," Thomas replied.

"Seriously? I didn't realize it was that many," a surprised Shaggy said.

"Maybe someone saw something. Why don't you ask around and see what you can find out. I'm going to look through his stuff for a clue about where he was and maybe where he went."

"Okay, but if you find anything worth selling, we split it 50/50."

"You are one cool customer, Shaggy, you know that? If I find something valuable I'll keep it safe so when Mike returns we can give it back to him."

"Whatever, bro," Shaggy said with a wave of his hand while he walked away.

Thomas sifted through Mike's things and discovered he'd done extensive research about child custody cases and according to his notes, it was not encouraging for a father who was homeless and out of work. Maybe that's why he didn't share what he found, or could there be another reason? Maybe Teen Wolf was lying in a ditch somewhere after a bookie wanted to make an example of him for others who weren't willing or able to pay up.

Thomas flashed back to his playing days when he first met Mike, a prominent attorney and a sports fanatic. Many of the players partied at a place called McGregor's, down the street from the stadium and the Chargers' training facility. Thomas was a fixture at the bar there (and there is even a plaque with his name on his favorite bar stool). Mike would always sit next to him and talk sports and ask intelligent questions. In hindsight, Thomas realized this was Mike's way of trying to figure out who was playing hurt or having off-field problems in order to get an edge when placing his next bet—yet despite the inside information, he still lost a lot more than he won.

When Mike's life began to unravel due to his degenerate gambling, he was desperate and turned to Thomas for a loan. It was a big misconception in the 1980s that professional football players were flush with cash. Most made a decent salary, but typically only in the upper-middle-class range. Plus, many were broke half the year because they only got paid during the season and didn't always manage their money well enough to last the other six months. Thomas did better than some, but it wasn't like he was living large. So, when he gave Mike what he had in his wallet at the time, it was more of a gift than a loan, despite Mike's insistence he'd pay it back.

To his credit, though, Mike offered Thomas free legal advice over the years when he could, as a way to pay back Big Mac's generosity. Mike even offered to help Thomas sue the NFL for disability payments, thinking it was a good bet he would win, but the two never got around to it. However, based on the custodial-rights book that Thomas discovered Mike had "borrowed" from the law library, it was clear Mike was still trying to make good after all these years. In the world of homelessness, this was a grand gesture, and Thomas made a vow to find his friend.

CHAPTER 4

"HEY BOSS, WHAT'S SHAKING?" RITCHIE Goldman asked Julie, his editor at the small community newspaper where he'd been a reporter for way too long. Based on his background and advanced degree, this job should have been a stepping stone, but instead it'd become his landing spot. In his parents' eyes, he was a huge disappointment. His mother would often call him and say—in her thick, Jewish, New York accent—"Ritchie, why don't you do something meaningful with your life? Your friends from school are all doctors and lawyers, and what are you doing out there in California? I'll tell you what you're doing, nuthin'. You're wasting your time with that *fakakta* job writing for that *pisher* of a paper. Come home and work for your father. You would be a wonderful salesman, even better than your brother Morty, who has zero personality. Oh, and Nancy Bergman is still single. I'm just sayin'."

Nancy Bergman wasn't his type and he much preferred his lifestyle out west to what waited for him back east (including his overbearing parents). Truth be told, his current girlfriend—like his mother—wasn't all that thrilled with his lack of ambition, either. For better or worse, she was sticking around with the hope she could change him into more of a go-getter. When Ritchie learned of her plan, he said to her, "I know what I want, and I have it delivered."

Ritchie was fine with what he was doing—writing fluff pieces about beach life. This simple, pressure-free lifestyle suited his laid-back and lackadaisical nature perfectly, and he was able to hang out at the beach and his favorite bar whenever he wanted.

Even though he was born a New Yorker, he always felt he belonged elsewhere—and California was it. His dorky glasses were now prescription sunglasses. His dark curly hair was now light brown, bleached by the sun. His skinny white legs were tanned to a dark chestnut color. His Bermuda shorts and white tank tops were replaced by surf trunks, aloha shirts, and flip-flops. His New *Yawk* accent was all but gone. He learned how to surf and used his baseball skills to compete in the annual over-the-line tournament on Fiesta Island. Then there was his weekly column in the paper. All in all, most everyone assumed Ritchie was a local.

"Ritchie, did you finish the piece I asked you to write about the sea wall repair for the online edition?" his editor asked, jolting him back to his present reality—a looming deadline.

"Uh, yeah, sure. It just needs a little polishing up before I submit it," he lied.

The fact was, he hadn't even started it but would bang it out as soon as he found inspiration sitting at his desk, or to put it more accurately, on a bar stool at Tug's Tavern—conveniently located right across the street from the paper's offices—which was where he was heading when he saw his boss and made the mistake of engaging her.

"Forget about that. I put the intern on it. What I need from you is another one of your 'Where Are They Now?' pieces. It's been..." Julie paused as she looked it up on her tablet. "... three months since the last one. Our readers really like those and I want your next one by the end of the week."

Ritchie just stared at her. Darn. Now he'd have to do some real research and writing. "Sure, boss. I'll get right on it." And off he went out the door of the offices of the *Beach and Bay News* to Tug's, where he bellied up to the bar and ordered a beer for breakfast while he waited for inspiration to strike. Four beers later, he had... nothing. But he wasn't as worried as he had been.

"Can I get you another one, Goldman, or are you working?" Bullet, the bartender asked Ritchie with a wink.

"That depends, Bullet."

"Okay, I'll bite. It depends on what? Whether you are driving, walking, or riding your bike home?"

"I'm walking, but that's not it. I need to find someone for my 'Where Are They Now?' series. Got any ideas?" the reporter asked the bartender, A while back, Ritchie had come in with the same dilemma and ended up writing about Bullet, who got his nickname when he was a patrolman in Chicago and got shot protecting a woman from her abusive husband. Fortunately, he was saved by his bulletproof vest. The guys on the force called him "Bulletproof" until he was shot a second time in the leg while breaking up a party. His nickname was shortened to "Bullet" and it stuck with him well after he retired early with a disability pension and began bartending to pass the time and drink for free.

"What about Skip? He's been shaping boards next door at Bird's Surf Shop for what, sixty years?" Bullet said while sweeping up a bit behind the bar.

"Don't let Skip hear you say that. He thinks he's still twenty. Besides, I already wrote about him a couple of years back when his wife ran for mayor. No, I need someone the readers would *really* be surprised to learn where they are now."

"You have readers? Huh," Bullet joked.

"That's just it. Julie is putting pressure on me to write things that will get people to pick up the paper and read it—and you know how well I respond to pressure," Ritchie said as he polished off his beer.

"Yeah, like the Chargers' quarterback, you choke," Bullet said and put a fresh, cold brew on the counter.

"The Chargers. Hmm... the Chargers. Bullet, you've lived here longer than me and you know a lot of the old players. Maybe one of them would make for a good article. What about that guy they called Bambi?"

"Lance Alworth? He doesn't live here any more. In fact, many of the greats are gone, but there is a guy who you could write about—but it's more of a riches-to-rags kind of story."

"That's okay. Who?" Ritchie asked and leaned forward for Bullet's answer, at the same time he subtly pushed his suddenly half-empty beer mug closer to the bartender. Bullet didn't bite on the refill.

"You ever hear of Big Mac?" Bullet asked.

"Thomas MacDonald, the lineman? Yeah, he's been in the news more than once."

"Yup. He's still around, but he's kinda homeless now."

"Didn't he get arrested for assaulting someone a while back?"

"Which time?"

"I remember a story about him being jumped by a bunch of bikers outside of Sasha's Bar and Grill and he sent all six to the hospital. They then tried to sue *him* for damages, but he was already broke by then."

"There is that. He's a scary-looking guy. He's really tall and has a dark unibrow and fierce-looking eyes. Add to that a crazy head of hair and long beard that make him look like a lumberjack and you have one mean-looking dude. If I was still a cop, I'd call for backup before even talking to him. The few times he came in here, he just sat at the bar with his head down. I don't think he ever said a word. He just glared at me from time to time and I'd give him another beer... on the house, of course. I never had any trouble with him, though, and from what I hear he's a really big teddy bear unless you make him angry. Then he's a grizzly bear with mad fighting skills. He studied karate or something, they say. Either way, a lot of people are afraid to talk to him. I know for a while he was banned from a lot of the bars at the beach because he would run up a tab and then leave, but nobody had the guts to stop him. But I didn't believe a lot of what was written about him, because it mostly came out of his divorce. Who knows the truth? I went through a nasty divorce myself, and my ex made me look like a really bad guy... which I'm not, just for the record."

Ritchie hadn't even heard the last couple sentences from Bullet's mouth—he'd already made up his mind to do the story and had his iPhone out to do a quick Google search on Big Mac. The more he read, the more he wanted to meet the man and find out more.

CHAPTER 5

"DAD, IT'S NOT LIKE I DON'T HAVE FRIENDS. I DO. I'm just not into what they're into," Abby said as she parked her pink bike next to her father's van and removed her book bag from the white wicker basket.

"And what are your friends into?" her father asked while fiddling with one of the straps holding down the patio cover in front of the van, not sure he really wanted to know.

"Boys."

Thomas stopped what he was doing and looked down. "What do you mean, boys? Like dating?"

"Dad, really. Get a grip. Nobody my age dates. We just, I don't know, hang out," Abby said while checking her phone for messages. There were none.

"Where do you hang out with these boys?" Thomas asked, now really sure he didn't want to know, but also sure he had to.

"I don't know because that's not what I do." Abby actually had no interest in boys, but she was having a little fun at her father's expense, though she knew it was probably a good time to stop.

"What do you do, besides hang out with your old man?"

"Read. I like to read... and write. I think I want to be a writer someday. What do you think?"

"Abby, I believe you could do anything you set your mind to, and if you say you're going to be a writer, then that's what you'll be. I have no doubt—and after you make it, there will be plenty of time to meet boys when you're, I don't know, say, thirty or forty," he said, trying to make it sound casual, but he wasn't kidding.

"Funny, but thanks, Dad. I won't disappoint you."

"I know, Abby. You never do."

Trying to avoid an awkward moment where the two would break down and cry, Abby threw her book bag over her shoulder and quickly added, "Speaking of writing, I'm gonna go in the van and start on my homework. I have a writing assignment that I have to polish up. It's due by the last day of school, which is only two days away. I can't wait!"

"Abs, what about your brother? What does he want to be when he grows up?" It nagged at Thomas that he had no idea what his estranged young son was into.

"I don't know, Dad. He doesn't talk to me all that much. I know he's been building hotels with his Legos and says he wants to be a developer," she said, not realizing it was the wrong thing to say until it was already too late.

"A developer. Really? I thought maybe he'd want to be a football player like his famous father. No, he wants to be a developer like his stepfather," Thomas said, spitting out the last word, *stepfather*. "It figures. But I'll tell you... I'm not having it."

The two were heading into the van when a red vintage Mustang convertible pulled up and parked right next to them. A skinny guy with Ray Ban sunglasses and a bright blue aloha shirt hopped out of the classic car without opening the door.

"Doesn't the door work?" Thomas asked.

"Yeah, it works, but jumping out is a much cooler way to exit the car, don't you think?" the kid said with a smirk.

"Not really," Thomas replied with a straight face. Upon closer inspection, the guy seemed older than Thomas had first thought.

The visitor pulled a notepad out of his pocket. "You're Big Mac, right?"

"Maybe. Who are you?"

"Oh, sorry, I'm Ritchie Goldman... you know, reporter for the *Beach and Bay News,*" the younger man said as he extended his hand.

Thomas towered over Ritchie and could have crushed his skinny little hand if he wanted to, but instead gave Ritchie a quick shake and walked around the Mustang. "This looks like a '65."

"You know your cars. It was my dad's and he passed it down to me just before he...." Ritchie halted as he unexpectedly choked up just a little.

"Well, he'd be proud of the way you've kept her up," Thomas said, having also lost his father at a young age.

"Thanks, I appreciate that."

Abby stretched out her hand and interjected, "Hi. I'm Abby."

Ritchie shook her hand and then thumbed through his notebook, searching for a blank page, poised to write. "Abby MacDonald?"

"Whoa, Ritchie Rich," Big Mac said sternly. "I'm not sure what your angle is, but whatever it is, my daughter is off limits."

Abby rolled her eyes and Ritchie smiled at her. "I like what you did with your 1974 Westfalia Camper Van, Mr. MacDonald. Can I go in?" Ritchie asked as he nodded toward the yellow Volkswagen.

"Abby is going to go inside and do her homework so we can talk out here," Thomas said as he pulled up a beach chair for Ritchie to sit in and gave his daughter "the look" that meant he was serious. She quickly headed inside.

"It was nice meeting you, Abby," Ritchie said as he sat down and got his pad and pen ready. A moment later, he turned to Thomas. "Okay, as you might've guessed, the reason I'm here is I want to interview you."

"Not interested."

"But you haven't even heard what I want to write."

"Not interested."

"I see. That's okay. I knew it was a long shot. I just thought you might have a message for the readers who remember you as a player and could learn from your experiences on the field and on the streets—especially the younger ones."

"Nice try, Ritchie, but the last thing I need is publicity. I'm trying to stay under the radar, in case you haven't noticed."

"All right, but can I ask you something—off the record?"

"You can ask, but whether I answer or not depends

on what you want to know."

"Fair enough. Is it true you were with the former Tampa Bay Buccaneer linebacker Marcus Dupree when he was shot and killed by police in Mission Beach?"

"Off the record?" Thomas confirmed.

"That's what I said."

"No, I wasn't with him."

"What about on the record?" Ritchie asked, with his pen at the ready.

"No, I still wasn't with him. We didn't get along."

"Huh, I thought I read somewhere you two played at the same time."

"Different positions, different teams. His job was to get to the quarterback and my job was to stop him. Outside of football, he was a horrible drunk." Big Mac slurped his rum and coffee. "I'm told I'm a joy to drink with."

"Who do you like to drink with, then?" Ritchie asked, pressing on.

"This is starting to sound a lot like an interview—which I think I already refused to do."

"You're right. Jeez, I'm sorry. Force of habit. If you ever do decide you want to talk, just let me know. I'm told I'm a good listener—and I'm also a joy to drink with," Ritchie said with a smile. He gave Thomas his business card and shook his hand. "Great to meet you," he added as jumped in his car—again without the benefit of opening the door. Thomas didn't reply, silently watching as the reporter drove off.

But he didn't drive far. He was intrigued by the former football great. Outside the entrance to the old campground, he parked and looked down at his pre-meeting notes. NFL.com listed MacDonald as 6-foot-5 and 310 pounds. *Well, maybe in his playing days,* Ritchie thought. The man he'd just met was still very tall, but he couldn't have weighed more than a couple hundred pounds. He looked terrible—dirty and disheveled—but he did look extremely fit. He made a note of that. It could be that his current lifestyle no longer included gourmet meals, or maybe he was one of the many players who had taken performance-enhancing drugs but then lost a lot of weight once they stopped. Ritchie remembered reading that Thomas competed in mixed martial arts competitions to earn money, so maybe he still trained for that. But more significant questions remained. Did his daughter live with him? Where was his son? Did his ex-wife get everything in the divorce? Were the awful allegations she made against him true? There was a story here; he just didn't know how to break the ice to get the former football star to open up. It was in that moment of thought that Abby rode by on her bike, headed to get a treat to help her finish her paper—and Ritchie had an idea.

CHAPTER 6

IF THERE WAS ONE THING SHAGGY LIKED ABOUT being homeless, it was the freedom to do what he wanted, when he wanted, and how he wanted—and who he wanted to do it with. People assumed his life was better when he was known by his real name, Ron, and worked at a big-box store as the resident expert on home-theater systems and manager of a small team of other electronics buffs. Even though Shaggy's boss endorsed a "Results-Oriented Work Environment" (ROWE), Shaggy had to be there 60 to 70 hours a week just to get the results his manager demanded. He made decent money, had all the latest and greatest gadgets, and was completely covered for medical and dental, but he was miserable.

Prior to working at the store, Shaggy had dropped out of school, but not because he couldn't cut it—he was plenty smart. What made it unbearable was the rigid schedule and teachers constantly telling him what to do. So, he joined the military, enticed by the TV ads promising adventure and a solid career.

As smart as he was, that was not a smart move. The TV ads didn't quite convey the rigor and discipline that would be expected of him. So, while he excelled as a communications technician, he failed as a subordinate. That he wasn't discharged from the Navy sooner was only due to how valuable his skills had become. His specialty was radar, and nobody was better at the job than he was. Conversely, nobody was worse at following orders and rules. He often ignored the very safety procedures put in place to protect him from the dangerous aspects of working with radar—and this led to his medical discharge. That he would never be able to have children due to exposure to high levels of radiation didn't factor in his disability compensation, but it should have, since being sterile greatly reduced his marriage prospects. So, as Shaggy grew older and increasingly dependent on alcohol, his monthly checks would only keep him afloat for a week or two before they were blown on food and booze—and not in that order.

It was natural, then, that Shaggy—when Thomas ordered him to ask around about some of the missing homeless—responded as he did to any other order, by doing the opposite. He was free to choose to do or not do what he wanted, and this time he chose "not do." Instead, he left the park and went walking along Riviera Drive, a road that ran right next to Mission Bay. It was a beautiful day and he watched boats sail past, propelled by the gentle sea breeze. He had that feeling he always got when he didn't do what was asked or expected of him. It felt like he was playing hooky—and as much as he was addicted to alcohol, he craved this feeling even more.

When the unmarked white panel van pulled up behind Shaggy and slowly trailed him for two blocks, he didn't think twice. When the van sped by and pulled over in a dirt cutout a block ahead, he just walked on. But when he noticed the van had no license plate and the sliding side door was open, he slowed his gait a little and checked the traffic to see if he could cross the street.

He stopped walking to wait for a passing car. At that moment, the van quickly backed up and when he was even with the open door, it was too late. Two masked men reached out and grabbed him by his jacket and pulled him toward the van. Shaggy instinctively fought back, letting the men pull the jacket off his body while he slipped and rolled onto the ground. One of the men was on him a split second later. Shaggy used a martial arts move Thomas had taught him and snapped the assailant's head back with a blow to the chin. This should have knocked him unconscious, or at least knocked him back, but the man remained firmly on top of him. Now he felt two gloved hands squeeze his neck... hard. He tried to pry the fingers from his throat, but Shaggy was not a strong man and couldn't get free. Swinging to hit the man, his arms only flailed uselessly. If he wasn't panicking before, he was now. He didn't want to die, but more importantly he didn't like someone else telling him it was time. Before Shaggy lost consciousness, the last thought that floated through his mind was that this was a major violation of his personal freedom.

CHAPTER 7

"COME ON, MAN, PUT YOUR BIKE IN THE BACK and I'll drive you home, no funny business, I promise," Ritchie said to Abby as she rode alongside his car on her beach cruiser, smartly refusing to get in.

"Stranger danger," she said, peddling away from the convertible.

"What?"

"You know, stranger danger. We're taught not to talk to strangers," Abby yelled back.

"I'm not a stranger. I'm a reporter," Ritchie replied when he caught up to her again.

"Oh, in that case," Abby said, tongue-in-cheek as she rode.

"Fine, but can we talk?" Ritchie pleaded.

"You mean, can you interview me about my famous father, and the answer is no. But…."

"But what?"

"I do have a story you may be interested in," Abby said as she slowed her pace.

"If it's about some middle school drama, I doubt I can get it published."

"Puleeze. You think I'm that shallow?" Abby asked.

"No. I, I don't know. How old are you again?"

"Old enough to know when a story has legs," Abby replied.

"Has legs, eh? So you know the lingo. Okay, I'm listening, but can we please stop so I can take notes?"

"Fine, meet me at Mr. Frosty in five minutes," and with that, Abby rode off while Ritchie was stuck at a red light in his vintage red Mustang convertible.

"I'll be there," the reporter yelled after her.

Ritchie pulled up and parked at the popular Pacific Beach ice cream shop that looked like it had been there since the turn of the century... the 20th century, when soft serve ice cream was first invented. He saw that Abby was already in line. He walked up and heard her order a double-dipped ice cream cone. "Want one?" she asked.

"Sure," he replied as Abby walked away leaving Ritchie to pick up the tab, a whopping five bucks.

They sat facing each other, eating their ice creams at the outdoor picnic tables in front of the local landmark, just a block from the beach, and enjoyed the cool sea breeze on the hot summer day.

"Aren't you going to take notes?" Abby asked.

"As soon as I finish my lunch."

"You need to take better care of yourself, mister, you're not a kid anymore," Abby said. "You could end up getting fat, like really fat."

Ritchie subconsciously rubbed his small paunch of a beer belly. He wasn't fat, but he wasn't fit, either.

"What do you know about the homeless situation in San Diego?" Abby asked.

"It's paradise here compared to living on the streets in someplace like, I don't know, Chicago or Detroit," Ritchie said as he licked a little bit of melted vanilla ice cream from his hand.

"Great, that's your take?" Abby said, feigning indignation.

"Well, no, but I'm trying to not let this cone drip all over me at the moment."

"What are your thoughts on the Mariner's Beach Park where my dad lives?"

"Who is interviewing who here?"

"Isn't it 'whom'?" Abby said with a raised eyebrow.

"Really? Really!?" Ritchie replied.

"Okay, let me ask you one more question," Abby said as she bit into her cone, finishing the top part of her ice cream without a drip. She was a Mr. Frosty's veteran. She and her dad used to come here on summer nights before her parents split and her world fell apart. Now her mom just gave her money and told her to go by herself. But it was more fun coming here with her father—in fact, everything was more fun with him. "What if I told you people were disappearing from the park where my dad lives?"

"Homeless people?"

"Yes, homeless people. Does that like make a difference? Are they not worthy of a story? Lots of them have been missing for months."

"Whoa. All I'm saying is these people don't have roots. Homeless people can come and go as they please, and they do. To say they are missing would imply they were found in the first place and according to a lot of people, they don't really exist—which is why we often look the other way or cross the street when one approaches us or is holding a sign asking for money. Abby, you know I'm right."

"So, let's change that. If we can find out what happened to these *people,* maybe someone will do something to make life a little easier for the *people* who are suffering on the streets of San Diego."

"I like your passion, Abby. Okay, tell me your story."

CHAPTER 8

JEFFREY WIENER HAD THE LOOK OF AN AGING rock star with his long hair pulled back in a ponytail, John Lennon-like glasses, goatee, goth leather jewelry, concert t-shirt, skinny jeans, and big boots as he stood tall (even though he was just over five feet, he looked larger) perched on a picnic table he began calling roll. It was something he'd been doing for the ten years since he'd found his calling and started coming down to Mariner's Beach Park to serve food to the homeless—and check in on them. After a rigging mishap on stage during a performance with his band in Austin, Texas—where a massive speaker fell on his head—Jeff sued and won a small fortune, but because of his injuries, his musical career was over. He used some of the settlement to buy a food truck and named it "Wok and Roll," from which he served made-to-order wok dishes and sandwiches on a roll. When the business failed, he decided to give his goodies away and that's when he stumbled on the park and the plight of its residents. He now had a cause and a purpose. He would serve meals on Saturdays and play his guitar for the all day "festival" of free food and good clean fun.

The rest of the week he was a tireless advocate trying to raise awareness for the homeless and raise funds by using his music business connections to get gear he could auction off. He was a good guy doing good deeds, but because of his last name, he was an easy target for some of the more unruly residents of the park to not-so-politely heckle him. His last name made it easy to pick on him—and the fact he was disabled and unable to defend himself didn't help, either. He didn't care. Many of the homeless had substance abuse issues, some were mentally unstable, and others just plain greedy and ungrateful, but he knew he was making a difference—especially with the teenagers who were new to the streets. In fact, one teenage girl who showed up with her guitar at the park one day knew of him from his band and asked for help with her career. He not only fed her, but he steered her in the right direction. She played area coffee shops and eventually landed a record deal, after which one of her songs suddenly and surprisingly became a big hit. How he helped people made him feel important and he held his head high like the hero he believed he was.

Thomas stepped in to calm the crowd, and with a wave of his enormous hand, the crowd was quiet. "Wiener is here to help you, so shut up or I'll make you shut up. Got it?" Thomas shouted, and everyone just nodded at the big man's request. "The floor is yours, Jeff."

Jeffrey cleared his throat, and began to call roll, using everyone's nickname instead of their real name—which he didn't know or need to know because nobody would answer to their given name anyway, even for free food. Anonymity was everything to the residents of the park for several reasons—most of them legal ones. He read his list in no particular order.

"Sunshine, Snaggle Tooth, Mad Max, Sandy, Rusty Nails, Dizzy, Whitey, Candy, Wookie, Stinky." As he read each name the person would nod or grunt they were there, and he would move on to the next name. "Pumpkin Head, Yoda, Big Unit, Pocahontas, Shooter, Red, Smokey Joe, Shaggy."

Everyone else was present up to the point Jeffrey called out Shaggy's name. After a few moments of silence from the group, Jeffrey asked, "Has anyone seen Shaggy today?"

"I kinda sent him on an errand," Big Mac answered, standing off to the side. "It shouldn't take him long. He'll be back soon."

Jeffrey shrugged and continued. "Cracker Jack, Teen Wolf."

Again, Thomas jumped in. "We haven't seen or heard from Mike, I mean Teen Wolf, in a while. You should ask some of your police buddies to keep an eye out for him."

Jeffrey made a note on a separate page where the names of other missing residents of the park were listed. It was a long list, and getting longer each time Jeffrey came around. He was both concerned and perplexed—where had everyone gone?

CHAPTER 9

"ABBY, WHERE *ARE* YOU?" ABBY'S MOM SLURRED her words while walking through the large one-level ranch house in her bikini with a glass of wine in her hand. "You better not be off spending time with your no-good father again or so help me God I'll ground you so long you'll be twelve years old before you see the light of day," she screamed.

"Mom, I *am* twelve years old," Abby said from behind the closed door of her room. "And I'll be thirteen at the end of this month in case you cared."

"Nobody likes a smart aleck, Abby. Especially me. Open this door. I want to talk to you."

Here it comes, Abby thought. Her mom was going to go on and on about some irrational issue and try to start a fight. It was sometimes hard to tell which of them was the adult. Her mom left her dad, but he would have probably left her eventually—nobody could put up with that kind of crazy for long. Her father would invent projects and go to his workshop in the garage for hours at a time and her mom would leave the kids alone in the house while she went out. Abby had to take care of her little brother and herself.

"I said, I want to talk to you."

"Mom, I'm doing my homework. I've been doing my homework all day."

"That's not what your brother told me. He said your bike was gone and so were you."

"What? He's just trying to get me in trouble again. Ask him if he's done *his* homework," Abby said through her closed door.

"Well if he hasn't, I need you to help him with it."

"Me? Why me?"

"Because you're not the one with friends and things to do."

Abby knew her mom was mean, but that was a low blow. It was true her brother and mother had more friends than she did. What they didn't have, though, was an amazing and wonderful person in their life like she had. They didn't have a relationship with her father, the absolutely best person in the world. He was her best friend, and she didn't apologize for it. Spending time with him was all she wanted to do—before and especially after what her mother did to him. So Abby opened her door, ready to give her mom a piece of her mind, but when she did her mother was gone.

CHAPTER 10

AFTER JEFFREY WIENER SHARED HIS LONG LIST of missing people, Thomas went back to his van and pulled a list of his own out of a hidden drawer under one of the seats. It wasn't a list of who suddenly disappeared from the park; it was a list of who would benefit from closing the park down by scaring away the residents. At the top of his very short list of suspects was one Donald McCallister, a developer specializing in hotels and golf courses who saw unlimited potential in a bay-front piece of property with easy freeway access and lots and lots of land. Thomas knew personally how calculating, controlling, and cold-hearted Mr. McCallister was since the jerk was now living with his ex-wife and kids.

McCallister wouldn't hesitate to eliminate anyone and everyone who stood between himself and a development deal. He'd steamroll public officials, politicians, and even the police if he could get his hands on a profitable piece of land—and the park would be as profitable as it gets. Dealing with a few dozen homeless people with no real rights to the property wouldn't require him to break a sweat, and the possible payoff was so sweet he would have a hard time being patient and waiting for the park to become his... taking the more legal route.

If McCallister had his way, he would shut off the power and water today, bring in bulldozers tomorrow and scrape the filth from the earth, including Thomas. McCallister knew Thomas was living there and that he was one of the reasons the residents were resisting leaving.

As for the negative publicity ousting people from the park would create, no problem. McCallister was already known as ruthless, relentless, and a real piece of work. In fact, by all accounts he seemed to embrace the gangster image and insisted everyone call him "The Don," partly because Donald Trump had already taken the title of "The Donald," but also because he probably saw himself as somewhat of a mob boss—doing what needed to be done and believing the ends did justify the means.

In a twisted way, McCallister told everyone his projects were good for the city, and on more than one occasion stated his opinion that the politicians in power and the minions they represented lacked real vision—which he believed he had in spades. If he made millions of dollars in the process it was a risk/reward proposition—the city took all the risks and he would reap the rewards.

The Don donated large sums of money to good causes, as evidenced by his name prominently displayed on a variety of public facilities, but not because it was the right thing to do. It was more to stroke his ego and convince others that he was a very important person in the growth of the city.

But knowing all of this didn't get Thomas any closer to figuring out how to prove it was McCallister and his cronies who were behind the disappearance of the people from the park—or how to get The Don out of the house Thomas had built and away from his kids.

Thomas cursed the day he first met the man. The owner of the Chargers was also a developer and brought The Don, his golfing buddy and business associate, down to the locker room to meet the team. The fact this meeting took place after a tough loss against their division rivals, the Raiders, made it more memorable. It was clear McCallister knew nothing about football as he greeted each player he met with a smile and handshake.

When he got to Big Mac's locker, Thomas still had his game face on and just stared down at him. Thomas was almost a foot taller and outweighed the man by over 100 pounds. Thomas was filthy, sweaty, and most of all, angry. He'd battled in the trenches all day unsuccessfully fighting off opposing players who would do anything to get an edge and crush his quarterback—and did. The Raiders were the most penalized team in the NFL, and for good reason. They played dirty, but when necessary (especially against the silver and black) Thomas got in more than his fair share of low blows and late hits—and not one flag flew his way. His hands were so quick from martial arts training he could get in under a player's face mask and jab him in the eye, nose, and his specialty—the throat—before the refs could see it. If the other player wasn't left incapacitated, he usually tried to retaliate and almost always ended up as the one being penalized for unnecessary roughness.

When he was on the field and in a game he became a totally different person, or did he? He wasn't a mean man by nature, but he did have a short fuse and under certain circumstances he would use his strength and speed to take down any man who tried to harm him or his family, including his football family. To say Thomas had anger-management issues was an accurate statement even back then. In his playing days, he was so juiced up he had a hard time shutting down what was clearly an asset on the field and a liability off of it—especially when you added alcohol and drugs to the mix.

So when Mr. McCallister came along and said, "Tough game out there. It looked like you got pushed around pretty good and your quarterback really took a beating today," Big Mac simply ignored the man's outstretched hand and jabbed him so fast in the throat that the people around him (including the owner) thought the newcomer was choking on something (other than his words) instead of having his windpipe partially collapsed by Big Mac's quick and crushing blow.

Was he sorry it happened? Yes and no. At the time it felt like the right thing to do—teach that idiot a lesson he wouldn't soon forget... and he didn't. After putting the developer down on the ground gasping for air and writhing in pain, Thomas simply walked away and took a shower as if nothing had happened. It was in his nature to right wrongs, and he could tell this guy was all kinds of wrong.

Today, he did things like that with a little more tact and thought. Then... not so much. Still, from time to time, Big Mac would bully a bully if that's what it took to balance things out and create a fair and level playing field. Looking back on that one quick reactionary response, of course he had regrets and would do it differently, because that one jab changed his life forever by creating an enemy for life.

A few days after the incident in the locker room, Thomas received a threatening letter from The Don's lawyers that included a rather rare request—a face-to-face meeting and an apology and all would be forgiven. Thomas blew the whole thing off until the owner of the team insisted Thomas make the time to meet the man... or else. Thomas didn't know what the "or else" threat meant, but he did know the owner wasn't going to cut him since he was a perennial All Pro. His agent and others reminded him that when the person who signs your paycheck makes a demand like that, it makes good business sense to at least listen. Everyone agreed to a meeting in the owner's office. When the owner's secretary, who was a fan of Big Mac, met him at the door, she told him to be nice and then gave him a pat on his butt as she ushered him into the expansive office where The Don and the owner waited.

As The Don began his diatribe, Thomas pretty much drowned out all the stuff about respect and controlling his rage until the owner got up and left the two men alone. That was the beginning of the end, as The Don explained how he would ruin Thomas and make it his life's mission to make Thomas's transition out of football a failure. He knew from his buddy, the team's owner, that Thomas had plans to start a construction company after his playing days were over. The Don said he would make sure Thomas never landed one bid to build anything bigger than a shed—and true to his word, McCallister made it very hard for Thomas to get his business off the ground when the time came. Fortunately, not everyone jumped when the demanding developer said so, since The Don had steamrolled many others on his road to the top. McCallister also reneged on his promise to drop the lawsuit if Thomas agreed to meet him in person—shortly after their meeting The Don sued Thomas for damages, and won.

Whether or not it was part of McCallister's original plan to steal Big Mac's wife and family away from him, it's what he did. The word "vindictive" comes after "venomous" and "vile" in the dictionary, but the man was a snake who would carry a grudge to the grave—and it was always the other guy's grave he carried it to. McCallister wasn't someone to be taken lightly. He had powerful allies, as Thomas came to find out when they finished him off, framing him for a series of small crimes he didn't commit in order to discredit the former football great. Thomas was crucified in both the legal court and the court of public opinion.

But his popularity as a player took the biggest hit when McCallister hired high-priced lawyers to help Big Mac's ex-wife paint a picture of Thomas as a monster in divorce court, accusing him of everything from being an unfaithful husband (untrue), a bad dad (absolutely untrue), and a violent and dangerous man (okay, that part was true, but his anger was never aimed toward his family). The public smear campaign was so thorough, even his own mother thought some of the things said about her son were possible.

In the end, Thomas was defeated and retreated to

the park with his van and not much else. That was almost three years ago, but the damage was done and it seemed impossible to get it undone. Thankfully, the people in the park didn't care about what others said about Big Mac. They judged him on who he was and what he did, and he did a lot... for them.

Thomas had killed McCallister many times in his mind—and gotten away with it. He had followed him, lay in wait, ready to murder the man with his bare hands, but in the end his love of his children prevented him from following through on his murderous impulses. He wanted McCallister dead, but if Thomas was convicted and incarcerated for his murder he would lose any chance of having a relationship with his son and daughter. No, he had to find a legal way to bury the man. He didn't care if he ever cleared his own name, but he had to discredit McCallister and do to him what he had done to Thomas—ruin his reputation and kill the man... figuratively, without having to lay a hand on him.

CHAPTER 11

"HEY BOSS, WHAT DO YOU KNOW ABOUT THE history of the homeless camp out on Mariner's point?" Ritchie asked his editor when he was next in the office.

"Why, you thinking of moving there, Ritchie?" Julie replied.

"Real funny. No, I'm happy with my cozy Mission Beach cottage, but with what you pay me...." Ritchie and his girlfriend lived in a little one-story place steps away from the beach for just over a thousand a month. It was a real find since it also had two parking spaces—akin to winning the lottery in Mission Beach.

"Don't even go there. Did you finish the 'Where Are They Now?' article I asked you to write?"

"Uh, um, what was my deadline for that again?"

"Today."

"By today, do you mean by the end of the work day, or the end of the day… like at midnight… Hawaii time?"

"Jeez, really Ritchie? What have you been doing all day?"

"That's just it. I went out to Mariner's Beach to interview a former Charger player for my article and I think I stumbled onto something bigger… better."

"Oh, no. Not again. You are *not* an investigative

journalist writing for the *Washington Post*. You write for a community newspaper filled with fluff pieces. It's what you do. It's what we do."

"What if we could break a big story… for once?"

"I don't know, Ritchie. Maybe, as long as it doesn't upset one—or all—of our advertisers. Lord knows we don't have enough revenue as it is. What'd you have in mind?"

"What if I told you that people were disappearing from the park never to be seen again?"

"Oh, come on. Really?" Julie rolled her eyes, slightly mad at herself for nearly falling for another one of Ritchie's investigative journalism ideas. "And I suppose the police are just ignoring this massive mystery that the *Union-Trib* has also somehow overlooked?"

"The police may not know. The *U-T* may not know. This is a homeless hideout, basically. Who's even paying attention?" Ritchie replied, his voice rising with excitement. "But get this… the encampment is a prime piece of real estate that would be a developer's dream. Maybe there's a connection."

"Well, is there?"

"I don't know, but with your permission, I'd like to find out."

"What if I don't give you my permission, Ritchie? Or should I call you Bob Woodward?"

"Well, like what Woodward and Bernstein did with Nixon and Watergate, I'm still gonna investigate and find out what's going on, no matter what."

"That's what I thought," Julie sighed. "I'll tell you what. Get the 'Where Are They Now?' piece to me by the end of the day—that's five o'clock our time—and you can go on your wild-goose chase for a week. One week. Then get back to writing about local beach business. Deal?"

"Deal!"

"So, did you interview that former football player?"

"No, but in the process I did find a story to write about. You're gonna love it, I promise."

"I'd better, because your little side project depends on it."

"Boss, have you ever thought about taking one of those compassionate-management courses offered by that guy who writes the guest column in our paper?"

"Get out of my office!" Julie barked. She enjoyed the friendly feud with her number-one staff writer.

Ritchie smiled at her mock bossiness and walked away feeling better about his occupation than he had in the past decade—when he first started as a reporter for the little local paper.

The first thing Ritchie needed to do was talk to Abby, but where would she be in the middle of the day on a Wednesday? In school, of course, but which one? Ritchie couldn't remember her exact age, so he reread his notes. *Abby's twelve years old,* he thought, *which meant she'd be in...?* He had no idea, so he Googled it and came up with the most likely answer being seventh grade. There was only one middle school in the area, so he hopped in his Mustang convertible and made his way there, only to discover that Wednesdays were half days and the students were all gone. So, on a hunch he headed to Mr.

Frosty, where they had met previously. There were plenty of middle-schoolers there, but no Abby. Ritchie then tried the public library, where a lot of kids went after school. No luck finding the young Miss MacDonald at the library. He would have to go to her home, something he'd hoped to avoid.

"Who are you again?" Don McCallister asked, even though he was holding Ritchie's business card in his hand.

Ritchie wanted to say, "Who are *you*?" but he knew the man standing in front of him was none other than The Don. Everyone knew what the developer looked like from his photos, which were regularly plastered in the social pages of the big daily newspaper—and some knew him by his reputation as well. Ritchie recognized the man and knew his reputation, so he decided to tread carefully.

"Sir, I am a reporter with the *Beach and Bay News*, the community newspaper delivered to your door each week. Abby expressed an interest in journalism and asked me if I would be willing to let her shadow me for a day to see what the life of a real reporter is like. That's why I'm here." Ritchie hoped that seemed as believable as it sounded.

"You do know she's only ten, right?" McCallister asked.

"Actually, she's twelve, sir. But yes, I am aware of her age and that she attends middle school. Feel free to call the paper and check up on me if you like."

"I think I will. Stay here." The Don shut he door

right in his face.

While Ritchie waited, he was surprised at how small the "big man" was in person. He seemed larger than life on television and in the numerous pictures he'd seen. And when he first came to the door, Don McCallister appeared younger than expected—but up close it was pretty obvious he'd had a great deal of cosmetic surgery. Ritchie was also a little taken aback that the man didn't know how old his only stepdaughter was—and that he'd missed by *two* years.

He started writing in his notebook when the door reopened. This time it was a woman who was standing there in a skimpy bikini. He took a guess it was Abby's mother, but with all the work she'd had done, trying to turn back time to when she was a teenager, he wasn't entirely sure. The woman in front of him had the same strange plastic appearance as the stars of *Housewives of Orange County*. Her lips looked like a duck's bill, her breasts were way too big for her body, and her face was pulled so tight it was hard to read her expression. What he did guess correctly was that this woman was not glad to see him—even if it didn't show on her face. He decided to break the ice with a quick quip.

"Hi, I'm Ritchie Goldman, a reporter with the *Beach and Bay News*, and you must be... Abby's sister."

"Really, that's the best you've got?" the bleached-blonde woman (with bleached teeth to match) said between gulps of white wine.

"No, but it seemed like the right thing to say."

"What do you want with my daughter?" Abby's mother asked, pointing one of her perfectly manicured fingers in his face.

"It's not what you think."

"You better hope not, because my husband has very powerful friends."

"You mean Big Mac?"

"What? No, my current husband, not that loser who lives in his van down by the river."

"Well, technically, he actually lives in a van down by the *bay*."

"You think you're pretty funny. Well, you can take your little comedy routine and get off my property."

"Before I go, can I ask you a question?"

"You just did. See, you're not the only clever one," she slurred.

Ritchie thought to himself, *Yes, but I'm the only sober one.* Instead he said, "This is a really nice house, but I would've thought you and The Don, I mean Mr. McCallister, would live in a mansion somewhere by the beach, maybe next to Romney's new place near Windansea."

"First of all, it's none of your business why we live here, but if you must know, it's the only home my kids have ever known and I want to keep it that way. My husband is planning to build something bigger someday, but for now this is home. My home, so please leave."

Ritchie walked back down the driveway and got into his car, opening his door this time instead of just jumping in. It was a good thing he did, because Abby was laying across the front seats.

CHAPTER 12

DON MCCALLISTER HADN'T COME BACK TO THE door because he was busy talking on the phone to one of his best buddies from high school, who also just so happened to be the County Sheriff.

"His name is Ritchie Goldman. He's a reporter for some small-time paper here in town," McCallister told his personal friend and professional ally.

"What do you want me to do, Don?" the Sheriff said in a tone that hinted he didn't want to get involved. His high school friend asked for favors often—and many of them meant bending the rules and risking his job.

"Have him arrested."

"For what? He didn't break any laws. My advice: don't sweat it. It could be he was there for the reason he said he was, to help Abby learn about being a reporter."

"I don't buy it. And even if it's true, what's a grown man doing running around with a twelve-year-old?" The Don was proud of himself for remembering Abby's real age this time.

"I'll do a background check on the guy if it makes you feel any better. Okay?"

"Thanks. Do that, and let me know if you find anything—and I mean *anything*."

"Consider it done, Don. And, uh, since I have you on the phone, I'm afraid I have some bad news."

"About the park?"

"No. It has to do with your son. I got word that he was picked up for drunk driving."

"What? When was this?"

"Last night. Apparently, he was driving around with the lights off late at night and got popped with a couple of his friends, the ones in the Bird Rock Band of Brothers. But it was your son who was driving."

"Why didn't he call? This could've been a public relations disaster for me."

"He didn't call you because he was never charged. I called in a favor and got him released on a technicality. He was stopped in La Jolla by the San Diego PD, which I don't have any control over, as you know, but I know enough people there that I could make it go away. He made me swear I wouldn't tell you, but I thought you should know considering what's at stake."

"You did the right thing, Smitty. I'll take it from here. I swear, that kid is going to be the death of me."

"At your age, I wouldn't talk like that."

"At my age? Hey, buddy, we were born in the same year."

"Exactly."

CHAPTER 13

SHAGGY WOKE UP IN TOTAL DARKNESS. HE HAD no idea where he was. What he did know was he felt terrible, and he was cold, very cold. He tried to reach up and rub his aching head and quickly realized he couldn't move his hands, or any part of his body. He was strapped down. He began to panic. This was his worst nightmare. He struggled against his restraints, but all he could move was his head, so he tried to raise it as far as he could and bumped it against something hard and metallic. He screamed, but all that came out was a muffled sound. His mouth was taped shut. *What is going on??* he thought. He was trapped. He began to think about who would do this to him, but he couldn't think of anyone who hated him enough to do *this*. For the next few minutes, he struggled as hard as he could, trying to break free. But the restraints and his injuries from the abduction were too much to overcome, and he passed out from the exertion.

CHAPTER 14

IF THERE WAS ONE THING THOMAS WAS SURE OF, it was that Don McCallister was somehow involved in the disappearance of his friends and neighbors. The more he drank the more he was convinced that The Don was doing something nefarious, and Thomas began imagining all the painful things he could do to torture the little man to get him to talk and admit his role in whatever it was that was going on—and something *was* going on.

Sitting alone in his van with a bottle of Tequila and plotting how to kidnap and kill The Don was not the best use of his time. He had already played out all the scenarios in his head hundreds of times in the past few years but never acted on them because he knew he would be the first one the police would question—even if they never found McCallister's body, which they might not. He had a plan to dispose of the corpse in the depths of the underwater canyon just off the coast of La Jolla while creating an alternate theory of the crime and a false alibi. The only way it would work is if he could be at two places at one time. Or... he could enlist the help of one of the many homeless military veterans in the park who would be more than willing to take out the man behind the disappearances of the other homeless vets.

That's when it hit him. McCallister wouldn't dirty his own hands with the details of making the homeless disappear. No, he would have help so if it ever came out what had happened, he would have a rock-solid alibi. *Who would he use to help him?* Thomas took another swig of tequila, but it didn't offer any insight. He popped a couple of pain pills and washed them down with another long draw from the bottle, waiting for that familiar buzz to take hold.

In times like these he found inspiration playing music, so he picked up his beat-up bass guitar. (He had to pawn his prized and quite valuable Rickenbacker 4001, the one he'd played when he was in a band with three of his teammates back in his football days.) Mostly, he played alone, but occasionally he'd jam with Jeffrey Wiener. Well, "jam" was a bit of a stretch—Big Mac couldn't afford an amp, so the two of them would hammer out 1970s classic rock songs at low volume levels. After noodling around for a bit, Thomas began playing "Roxanne" by The Police when the ray of an idea started to appear through the clouds in his mind. *Why hadn't the police been involved in the search for the people who had disappeared?* Thomas assumed Jeffrey had been reporting the missing residents, but maybe he hadn't. It was time to find out what the activist had done… or not done.

CHAPTER 15

"WHOA. WHAT THE HECK ARE YOU DOING?" Ritchie asked when he nearly sat on Abby's head.

"You've got to get me out of here. Please," Abby pleaded.

"Not a good idea. I can write my own headline for this sad story: 'Reporter Arrested for Taking a Joy Ride With Twelve-Year-Old Girl.'"

"Okay, then let me drive," Abby said, not exactly kidding.

"You can drive? Don't answer that. I don't want to know. There is absolutely no upside for me going anywhere with you."

"What if there's a story in it? A big story," Abby said while still crouched down in the front seat of Ritchie's car.

"I'm listening."

"Don't you think it would be worse if my mom found me down here?" Abby pointed out, too young to grasp the implication in Ritchie's mind. "Can't we just go for a drive around the block?"

"Won't your mother know you're gone?"

"No. She's passed out by the pool, and my stepdad creeps me out, so I lock myself in my room all the time to avoid him, so he won't have a clue. Plus, I recorded a really long one-sided phony phone call recently, put it on a loop and I'm playing it on my computer speakers right now. I climbed out of my window, and here I am."

"Clever."

"You know it. So, can we get out of here?"

"Against my better judgment, we can park down the street and talk. In the future, here's my card, so just call me, okay?"

Abby took the business card, entered his number in her phone and handed it back.

"You're not going to keep the card?"

She stared at him until he got it.

"Ah, no connection other than your phone, which I'm sure you have ways to hide any calls or text messages."

"I learned how to cover my tracks since my mom and stepfather won't allow me to have any contact with my dad."

"Clever."

"You already said that. Can we go or what? Don't you think it looks kinda conspicuous, you sitting here talking to yourself?" Abby asked, still crouched down and out of sight on the floor of the passenger side of the Mustang.

"How old are you again?" Ritchie asked, already knowing the answer but not believing it.

"Old enough to know I don't have all day to tell you what I need to tell you."

Now that they were parked a few doors down, Abby laid out what she'd learned from her father, talking to other people at the park, and based on her own assumptions and research. Ritchie took it all in and took copious notes before he finally spoke.

"If what you say is true, and I believe you, then this is a conspiracy to acquire and develop the land by your stepfather. It makes sense, but there are some holes in your hypothesis. Simply systematically removing a few of the residents from the park won't help him gain control of the land."

"It's more than a few people who have gone missing. According to my dad, there are more than a dozen people who have vanished in the past few months."

"Your dad has a list of who has disappeared?"

"He does, and so does Jeffrey Wiener."

"Who?"

"There's a guy who comes to the park a couple of times a week to count the homeless, and he gives them food, water, blankets, and other stuff for free," Abby informed the reporter.

"I need to talk to him."

"Great, let's go."

"Nice try. I'll find him and see what he knows."

"There's more," Abby said. "I overheard my stepdad talking on the phone about the park. He knows my dad lives there, and I think taking the last thing my dad has left in life is part of my stepfather's plan to completely destroy him."

"Interesting. So he kills two birds with one stone, so to speak. He gets his hands on one of the last waterfront pieces of property to build something big and profitable, and he forces your father to find another place to live… possibly on the streets or somewhere dangerous.

It makes sense."

"So how do we prove it?"

"We know your stepfather has the means and motive to pull this off, so why hasn't it happened yet?" Ritchie asked, thinking out loud. "Assuming your theory is correct, we need to find out what's standing in his way, then we can guess what his next move will be and be ready for it. I've got a lot of work to do."

"What about me?"

"I know I'm going to regret asking this, but does your stepfather have a home office?"

"Yeah, it was my dad's, but my stepfather stripped everything off the walls and replaced all of my father's football photos with new ones of himself with a bunch of local legends and powerful politicians."

"Can you get in there?"

"It's locked, but I know how to pick the lock."

This time Ritchie just stared at *her*.

"Don't ask," Abby said.

"Believe me, I won't. If it's safe, and I mean safe, get in there and take photos of the pictures on the walls and send them to me."

"Should I go through the papers on his desk? Copy the files on his computer? Look through his trash and search for clues?"

"Calm down. That sounds way too risky right now. Just send me the photos, okay?"

"Okay, fine," Abby agreed.

They both knew Abby wouldn't stop with the photos, but neither said another word as both of their minds were spinning with the possibilities. Abby seemed excited to solve the mystery and discredit The Don just like he had done to her father. Ritchie wanted to solve the mystery and break what would be the biggest story of his sad career, but first he had a deadline to meet.

CHAPTER 16

JULIE LOOKED UP FROM HER COMPUTER SCREEN with tears in her eyes. "Ritchie, this is an amazing piece of writing."

"I know," Ritchie said with a straight face.

"How did you pull this together so fast?" his editor asked.

"I had some help. There's a guy named Jeffrey Wiener who knows everything there is to know about homelessness in San Diego. I met with him this afternoon and he had everything I needed to write this story."

"You know what would make this even better?" Julie asked.

"Let me guess. A photograph?"

"Exactly. That, and fixing all of your punctuation problems."

"You fix the punctuation and I'll provide the photo. It turns out Jeffrey shoots powerful pictures. Take a look at these," Ritchie said as he handed his editor a stack of black-and-white photos featuring several different people from the park.

"I like this one," Julie said, pointing to a picture looking into the vacant eyes of a homeless man with a beanie on his head, his long and wild hair sticking out and partially covering his equally straggly gray beard. "Is he one of the people in the article?"

"Julie, all of the people in these pictures are missing."

"What? All of these?" she asked as she thumbed through more than a dozen different faces. "Ritchie, I think this is too good for your column. This is front-page material."

"I agree, but I have something bigger and better planned for that. For now, run this as another 'Where Are They Now?' and I'll start working on the other thing right away."

"Are you going to tell me what this is all about?"

"Right now, the less you know about what I'm up to, the better."

"Okay, but please don't make me sorry I hired you all those years ago. The paper can't afford another lawsuit."

"It's good to know you've got my back, boss."

"Always, as long as you don't screw up."

"I know what I'm doing. This is just the first step."

"I trust you, Ritchie," Julie said.

"You're the best," Ritchie replied.

"You always say that."

"Well, 'Best' *is* your last name."

Ritchie left and Julie started to reread and edit the article, which was her job—one of many. The small newspaper was really run by her, with the help of a very small staff of young, dedicated people who believed in the power of the press—but who also wanted to get some good experience so they could move on to bigger and better jobs in journalism. Ritchie was the oddity. He wasn't a young man any longer, and he didn't seem to have any aspirations beyond what he was doing now, despite the constant nagging from his longtime girlfriend—now one of Julie's closest friends since she'd split with her husband. In the divorce, she got the newspaper and he got the house and everything that went with it. Julie believed *she* got the better deal. If success truly is the best revenge, then Julie was getting the last laugh. The paper was now on a successful upswing, and she looked better than ever as a fit and fashion-forward forty-something.

Julie smiled as she read Ritchie's work. She would have to share an advance copy with his girlfriend because this proved what they both knew, that he was a wonderful writer when he put his mind to it.

WHERE ARE THEY NOW?
By Ritchie Goldman, Reporter
Beach and Bay News

Admit it, when you see a homeless person on the streets of San Diego you avert your eyes, glad for your own good fortune and unwilling to share it with someone you probably believe will just spend it on booze. It's okay. There are 10,000 people in San Diego who don't have a home, and many of them live right here at the beach. However, there are fewer and fewer homeless living by the bay recently, but nobody seems to know why.

According to Jeffrey Wiener, an advocate for the homeless people, over a dozen people have seemingly vanished from the Mariner's Beach Park, a makeshift community of people with nowhere else to go. In this installment, it seems fitting to write about and truly wonder, "Where

Are *They Now?" Here is a little bit of background about each of the people who are no longer around for us to listen to their life stories and learn valuable lessons from their misfortunes.*

The article went way over the original word count as Ritchie wrote about each of the people who were no longer around. In just a couple of sentences for each person, Ritchie did an amazing job of respectfully putting a face and name to the missing people from the park. It was fascinating to learn about the background of the people who were gone. Many were military veterans and heroes, several were once married with kids, there was a doctor and a lawyer, and to Julie's surprise, a former writer from one of the now-defunct community newspapers she and her ex-husband had to close when advertising dollars dried up. She wondered, how close was she to being homeless? A bad deal, a poor choice or two away from losing it all?

CHAPTER 17

THOMAS WAS UNABLE TO FIND JEFFREY WIENER to ask him if the activist had been reporting the missing homeless people to the proper authorities. He assumed Jeffrey had, but he wasn't about to walk into a police station and ask if they knew about a bunch of anonymous and basically invisible people who were disappearing without a trace. On the other hand, if this had been reported, why hadn't any police or detectives come to the park to look into it? He needed to think this through, so he grabbed his longboard and walked the short distance to the beach.

The park was conveniently located between the beach and the bay. For him, the biggest decision he faced many days was whether to walk left or right out of his van. Left, and he could walk along the calm waters of the bay. Right, and he could head out to his favorite surf spot in the ocean. Walking along the path to the beach, he passed several empty spots where the camps of the missing once were. What was going on? He had to figure it out.

Paddling out for a surf session on a warm summer day *almost* made him forget his many problems. The waves were a fun two to three feet high and the water was a comfortable 72 degrees. Ducking under a couple of waves to get out to the lineup washed away the dirt from the days before and cleared his mind just a little. He made it outside the break and sat on his board taking it all in, trying to focus on the positives—he was relatively healthy, he had a special relationship with his daughter, and he had the freedom to be out here surfing on a weekday with nobody else around.

A lazy wave rolled in and he turned and paddled for it, quickly feeling the familiar rush of the water swelling underneath his board as he stood up and glided along a glassy peak, dragging his hand as he raced down the line of the perfectly peeling left without a care in the world.

After riding a dozen waves all the way to the beach, he was in the zone—catching the good ones and letting the little ones go by. In between rides, he looked down through the crystal clear water at his shadow on the sandy bottom six feet below. That's when it hit him. He was looking at the problem from his perspective instead of looking at it from The Don's point of view. All he was thinking about was the what, where, and when. What happened to his friends and neighbors, where did they go, and when were they last seen? He should be asking himself, *why* would they suddenly disappear and *who* would benefit from them leaving?

If he were a petty, greedy, powerful person like The Don, what would he do? First and foremost, he would want revenge on his number-one enemy (Thomas) and to bury him once and for all. But why not just come after him? Maybe he knows it wouldn't be that easy. Thomas would put up a good fight and point the finger at the one person who was probably responsible if he survived. McCallister would know Thomas' one weakness was his kids and his friends, but he couldn't go after his kids because their mom would dump him. Going after his friends and forcing him out of his "home" would be enough of a motive to explain what was going on. Was he offering people at the park cash to pick up and move? The City had a program that would pay a homeless person to move back home (as long as it wasn't in San Diego), so it seemed plausible, but probably not likely. No, the guys would have come back for their belongings and to say goodbye—and tell others there was free money for moving. If it were just two or a few people who had vanished, maybe. No, there had to be another reason.

What about greed? If McCallister could get his hands on this property he could put in a hotel, homes, and a whole host of other commercial options that would make him tens of millions of dollars. If enough people were removed and it was viewed as an unsafe place to live, maybe the city would come in and cut off the power and water and then kick the rest of the residents out. That this was an election year also meant the two leading candidates would not want to be seen as heartless by campaigning to displace a bunch of homeless people and force them to live in the streets, alleys, and parks of the surrounding neighborhoods. For the sitting mayor, this would be a good time to quietly make a move since he was termed out and leaving office. He could do it without any political fallout. Plus, McCallister could set him up with a cushy job in his company. So why hadn't the mayor closed the park?

Certainly The Don had the political pull to push people out and a good reason to do it—for greed and revenge. What was Thomas missing? He needed to talk this through with someone who was better connected than he was. He needed to talk to that reporter with the Mustang. *What was his name?* Thomas picked a wave out of the set coming in and rode it to the beach. Unknown to him, standing in the sand was a team of three ready to take him by force.

CHAPTER 18

IF THE HOMELESS PEOPLE KNEW THAT JEFFREY lived in a home overlooking the beach they would likely question his motives for his dedication to their cause and then roll him for his fat wallet. Wiener's reasons for devoting his life to helping others less fortunate was part of his penance for being such a schmuck after his tragic accident on stage. The money he made from the lawsuit and insurance claims helped him pay cash for his place, yet he spent his time at the camp and on his most important calling—feeding the homeless and building a home for at-risk teens who had run away. Before that, he had been an annoying pest to politicians, the police, and the press. He went from selfish to selfless and never felt better—even though he was in constant physical pain. The only thing that seemed to ease his suffering was taking long walks on the beach. And this is exactly what he was doing when someone suddenly hit him over the head and dragged him into a white van waiting by the sea wall, well out of sight of the other beachfront homes. The van drove off with Jeffrey inside, heading towards its final destination, a three-story building a few blocks over and tucked away on a side street in La Jolla.

CHAPTER 19

RITCHIE HADN'T FELT THIS GOOD SINCE… WELL, he couldn't remember. He just nailed his last article and was working on a story that could make a difference. For once he wasn't writing about the opening of a new pizza place—or the closing of another one. This was important. This mattered. Just then he started to doubt himself, as he always did. Who did he think he was? A real reporter? Not in years. Not ever. Writing puff pieces was what he did. His dad was right; he wasn't going to amount to anything. He had a terrible work ethic, no talent, and worst of all, he was a screw-up. Ritchie tried to shake his head to make the voices stop, and they did… but they were just replaced by his girlfriend's incessant nagging. She was a lot like Ritchie's father, who subscribed to the philosophy that if you had nothing nice to say, say it anyway.

The best way to shut out the chatter in his brain was to turn up the music in his Mustang, so he cranked up the radio. Unfortunately, the song was Led Zeppelin's "All Of My Love" about the death of Robert Plant's young son. Jeez. He quickly turned that off and started to think about what he was up against—a powerful group of people who could crush him if they wanted to, and they'd want to if he wrote what he was planning to. Maybe he should just scrap the whole idea and go back to what he did best, which was next to nothing.

As Ritchie wallowed in self doubt, his phone rang. The first call was from Big Mac. He left a voicemail that he wanted to meet. *Wow, I didn't see that coming,* Ritchie thought. Then his phone rang again. This time it was Abby, who also left a message about wanting to meet. He *did* see that one coming. The smart thing to do would be to call the father back and not his twelve-year-old daughter, but he never did the smart thing, so why start now?

"I have the pictures," Abby said immediately when she answered.

"Anything interesting?"

"I'm not sure, but I did find a few other things in my stepdad's office I know you will find interesting."

"Okay, how about I swing by tomorrow and see what you have?" Ritchie asked.

"Uh, I have school."

"Right, I forgot. Are you going to your real dad's after school?"

"Yeah, probably."

"Good, I need to talk to him, too. Why don't you meet me there at, say, I don't know, one o'clock?"

"You know, for a reporter, you don't seem all that sharp. School ends at two-thirty. I can be there by three or I can meet you at Mr. Frosty at two forty-five—a girl's gotta eat," Abby said, all adult-like.

"Nice try, but I'll meet you at the park. Like you said, I'm not getting any younger and I could stand to lose a few pounds."

"Okay, then. See you tomorrow... at my dad's," Abby said and hung up.

CHAPTER 20

THE SMART THING TO DO WAS USE HIS surfboard to smack the first guy and then hit the other two in quick succession, but Thomas wasn't willing to risk a ding to his custom ten-foot Donald Takayama longboard. It was a gift from a grateful quarterback and something he was reluctant to sell no matter how much he needed the money. Instead he gently placed the board on the sand, all the while pretending he didn't notice the three idiots preparing to jump him. The first thing that gave these guys away was how anxious they looked leaning against the sea wall along the boardwalk dividing the beach from the street. They appeared about as ready for a day of fun in the sun as a hockey player… from Canada… in full gear… in Miami… in July. These bozos were wearing long pants, blazers, and dress shoes while standing in the sand. Thomas had the advantage since he was barefoot, bigger in both height and weight, and a martial arts master.

After dropping his surfboard, Thomas quickly approached the man in the middle, figuring he was the leader. As he drew near, the man on the right reached behind his back, probably to grab his gun. Thomas was on him so fast, though, that the guy didn't even get his hand all the way back—it was now locked in a precarious and painful grip, causing him to drop to his knees and scream. Simultaneously, Thomas threw sand in the eyes of one of the other men as the third put his hands up to indicate surrender.

"Mr. MacDonald," the one with his hands up said, "we only want to talk to you, that's all. We're with the FBI."

Thomas didn't wait to check for credentials; instead he threw a quick strike with his free hand into the man's sternum, which took his breath away… literally. He fell to the sand gasping for air. Thomas then turned his attention to the man he'd blinded with sand seconds earlier and subdued him with a blow to the side of his head.

He searched the pockets of the man he was still holding in a one-handed death grip and found, much to his surprise, a badge of sorts. He flipped it open and, unless this was some kind of sensational forgery, all indications showed he was about to break the arm of a real-life G-man, so he let him go. The agent was in tears and still incapacitated from the pain, so Thomas felt safe checking the pockets of the other two—after he turned each one of them over so they wouldn't die from being face down in the sand. They too had FBI credentials. Thomas stood up, threw the badges near the bodies, picked up his board, and casually walked away. He wasn't about to stick around so he could be arrested and interrogated. They knew where to find him if they wanted to talk. Only this time he would be more careful... by not being there when they came to the camp.

CHAPTER 21

RITCHIE ARRIVED AT THE EMPTY CAMPSITE FIRST. Thomas's van was gone and so were some of his possessions. Stapled to the storage shed the big man had built when he "moved in" was a notice from the city of San Diego stating that water and power would be shut off and a deadline was set to vacate the park before it was to be leveled in two weeks. Ritchie ripped it off the wood and put it in his pocket.

As he looked around, people in the park were beginning to pack up their belongings and head for the hills, so to speak. Ritchie imagined the displaced would likely head to the beach rather than the nearby foothills, and this would be a big story unto itself. As much as that story needed to be told, Ritchie was more concerned about where Thomas might be, and whether his daughter knew anything about what was going on. While Ritchie waited for Abby to show up, he called the one person he figured would know what was happening. But Jeffrey Wiener's cell phone went straight to voice mail.

Abby rode up minutes later and simply dropped her bike and ran to the spot where her dad's van had been parked for the past two years. "I don't understand. He wouldn't just leave like this. No way. Was there a note for me?"

"No note, but there was this," Ritchie said, and handed Abby the eviction notice posted by the City.

Abby read it and then read it again. "This can't be happening. Not now."

"We had to see this coming. What did you find out when you were in your stepfather's office?"

Abby handed Ritchie her phone and said, "Scroll through the pictures and pay special attention to the photos of the plans I found in a locked drawer in his desk." At this point, he was no longer surprised that she could and would get into a locked anything.

Ritchie scrolled through the pictures, immediately recognizing the power players from San Diego politics, posing with a smiling Mr. McCallister in framed photos proudly displayed on the wall. Interestingly, the current mayor was in more than one of the snapshots, and so was one of the current candidates. Ritchie was deep in thought when he handed Abby her phone back—which she refused.

"You didn't go far enough. Keep scrolling," she told him.

Ritchie went past the pictures of other famous and some infamous locals on the wall including the sheriff and police chief when he got to what Abby wanted him to see—a series of pictures that looked like the master plans for the development of the park where they now stood.

"This makes sense. Of course. Your stepdad... "

"From now on, let's just call him Don, okay?" Abby said.

"Sure. This looks like *Don* has had his eye on this prized piece of property for a long time. If you look closely, the plans are dated two years ago. He's probably been pushing politicians and pulling strings so he could team up with the City to rid this place of the people living here—illegally, I might add—so they could break ground on this project."

Abby looked dejected. Ritchie figured it was not only about the people that would be displaced, but also the realization that the devil was living in her house and married to her mom—not to mention her father was now also among the missing.

Ritchie tried to cheer her up. "These plans don't mean much. Anyone can put together a proposal to purchase city-owned property. It doesn't mean they can or will get it."

"Keep scrolling," was all Abby said in reply.

Ritchie kept scrolling past the plans and there was a picture of a letter from the mayor and the City Council endorsing his new planned community and praising The Don for donating a portion of the land back to the city as a public park. The park would be built only after all of the other development was done.

"Ha. I've seen this movie before and I know how it ends," Ritchie started, "and it's not how it's scripted here. A new mayor is elected and all bets are off. Somewhere there is fine print in the agreement and suddenly the terms change—no public park if this or that happens, which Don the developer would make sure happened. The problems would then be blamed on the past mayor and council members who have already moved on to bigger and better things, and the public park is out and more homes are mysteriously built in their place." Ritchie shook his head in slight disgust at yet another political machination at the expense of good people.

Now it was Abby's turn to raise the spirits of the jaded reporter. "It looks bad, but like you said, this isn't written in stone. I did a little research and I couldn't find one article about this deal in the archives of any of the local newspapers... yours included. Don't you think this would have to be made public if a deal was done?"

"True. There would be public hearings in addition to the private meetings between the politicos and your stepfather... I mean, 'Don.' Now I'm just talking this through, but why did it take over a year to get this approved in principle? Look at the date of the plans and now look at the date of the letter. They're a year apart—the letter is dated almost a year ago."

"Since I do live with Don—yuck—I can tell you from firsthand experience he's not a patient person, so you make a really good point. I will say, this wasn't the only set of blueprints I found in his desk. He's looking to develop other stuff all over town. I found over a dozen different sets of plans, and this one was on the bottom."

"Interesting," Ritchie said, again lost in thought. Then it hit him. "We have to find your father."

"You don't think... " Abby said, not finishing the thought.

"Yeah, I do think there is a good chance your dad is going after your stepfather, which would end badly for both of them."

CHAPTER 22

BEING KEPT IN THE DARK, LITERALLY, SHAGGY hadn't seen the light of day since he was grabbed by the side of the road and thrown into the white van. Whoever was holding him hostage had stripped him of his watch—and his clothes—and left him locked in what seemed like a cold, metal, coffin-like box. He was unable to move, the strong restraints holding him firmly in place, and had lost all sense of time. He was sure he had suffered some kind of trauma to his head, as he was feeling slightly nauseous and didn't feel like eating—not that the kidnappers had offered him any food or water. Shaggy desperately needed a drink, but water wasn't the first thing that came to mind.

A door at his feet opened and Shaggy was slid out into a bright room. The overhead lights fried his eyes. When he was able to open them again, he looked around the large space and couldn't believe what he was seeing. He first thought he was in a hospital, because there was a set of overhead lights that looked like they belonged in an operating room. There was also medical equipment all around, and the people looking down on him wore surgical masks and scrubs. But something was off.

Two tables he could see in the center of the room

looked more like something in a morgue. They were metal and had drains in the center. When he craned his head and looked back, fear gripped him as he realized he had been held in a sliding steel storage space used for corpses. He *was* in a morgue. What the heck was happening? With his mouth taped shut, he couldn't ask where he was or why he was there, but he tried anyway. All that came out were unintelligible muffled sounds.

"Did you forget to sedate this one?" one of the masked men casually asked the other.

"No. It could be the drug doesn't affect him like the others. Let me make a note of that," he said and stepped out of view.

"Man, this guy is skinny. How long do you think he'll last?" the first masked man asked.

"Not long, that's for sure," the other one called back from elsewhere in the room. When they grabbed him, he looked healthier because he had on several layers of clothes. "I doubt they would've wanted to use him if they'd known he was this malnourished."

"We better not waste time then. Let's start the testing right now."

Shaggy kept trying to talk with them and used his eyes to plead for mercy. He doubted they were doctors, but one of them was now holding a large needle and getting ready to stick it in him.

"This is a lot easier when they're unconscious," the masked man holding the needle said to the other.

Shaggy struggled against the restraints, but one of the masked men climbed on top of him to stop any movement at all, while the other stuck the needle in. Shaggy immediately felt a strange but pleasant sensation as the drug raced through his veins. He closed his eyes and let it wash over him. *Ah, that's better*, he thought.

One of the masked men said to him, "Feel better now?"

Shaggy tried to nod his head yes, but it didn't move and not because of the restraints. It was something else. He tried to blink, but his eyelids wouldn't work. He made an effort to wiggle his toes, nothing. His brain sent a signal to flex his fingers, but they didn't respond. Whatever they gave him left him awake, but paralyzed from head to toe. He couldn't even feel them sliding him back into the dark chamber, but when the heavy metal door slammed shut, he knew one thing for sure—he wasn't dead, but he wished he were.

CHAPTER 23

"HI, SIS, YOU'RE LOOKING GOOD," SAID ABBY'S stepbrother Ron with a twinge of sarcasm when she walked in the door.

"What are you doing here?" she asked in complete surprise. "Did something happen to your dad?" Her stepfather had forbidden his only son from entering their house. She didn't know if they ever met elsewhere, but Ron wasn't supposed to be here.

"Why, did your psycho father finally do something to him?" Ron goaded her, knowing how she worshipped her real father.

It certainly was possible, she thought, but Abby was relieved to hear that Ron was in the dark—that was a good sign. "No, my dad didn't do anything to your father, but he should have a long time ago after your—"

"That's enough, you two," Abby's mom said as she entered the room. "Ron is here because I asked him over. I want him to help your brother with football. Alex is playing flag football over the summer and needs to practice."

"What about Dad?"

Abby's mother just stared at her.

"Really, Mom. Dad played in the NFL and Ron never played a down of football in his life." Her stepbrother was famously lazy and, as she examined him more closely, he looked completely out of shape. For a guy in his early twenties, he was slouched, soft, and looked like he hadn't seen a gym since junior high.

"That's not true, Sis. I played football in school."

"You played high school football?"

"No, I played in middle school, and I was a pretty good special teams player."

Abby just shook her head and walked away toward her room.

Abby's mom called after her, "Come back here, young lady. It's rude to just walk away in the middle of a conversation."

Abby stopped in the hall and stared back at her mother, wondering how she could have come from her genes. "I was done conversing, *Mom*. Besides, it seems like you've already made up your mind, so what more can I say?" There had been a lot of tension between the two after Abby's mom left her father. And it wasn't long after the breakup that The Don had moved in and acted like he owned the place. Thankfully, her mom had never required her to make nice with her new stepbrother... until now.

"Your stepbrother is a busy man. He and some of his friends are starting a company, and the fact he's willing to take the time to teach Alex about football says a lot."

From what Abby had heard, the only business her stepbrother could possibly be in was the drug business, but she bit her tongue and instead played along. "What kind of business are you starting up, Ron?"

"A none-of-your-business kind of business. Your mom knows all about it and she is even one of our investors. That's all you need to know."

Ron was all smiles. In fact, her mom and Ron were smiling at each other in a weird way. Abby tried to not think about what that might mean and instead asked, "Has anyone seen The Don today?"

"What did I just say about being disrespectful, Abby? You will address your stepfather as Don or Dad, but never call him 'The Don.' Is that clear?"

"It's okay," Ron said. "She can call me 'The Ron' if she wants."

Abby just shook her head at the absurdity of it all. This was her family, and the word *dysfunctional* didn't do justice to describe how messed up it truly was. "So nobody knows where *Don* is?" she asked again.

"Probably playing golf at the club," Abby's mom answered. "Why are you suddenly so interested in where your stepfather is?"

Abby didn't want to tell the truth, that she secretly feared her real father was about to pummel her stepfather... or worse. "I just thought Don didn't want Ron in our house."

Ron gave her a look that made her skin crawl. She could see in his eyes that he wanted to hurt her, which was one of the reasons he wasn't allowed to come around. There was something not quite right about Ron, and to her stepfather's credit, he knew it too. Don tried to protect Abby and Alex by banning his only son from family functions and visiting their house. It figures her mom would be the one to invite him over. She was beyond clueless.

Ron ran with a gang of rich kids who liked to cause trouble in the otherwise quiet beach community. They called themselves The Bird Rock Band of Brothers, named for the Bird Rock neighborhood in La Jolla. More than once, the phone rang in the middle of the night and her stepfather had to go and bail Ron out of jail. Other times, when Ron called the house, her stepfather either refused to talk or belittled him on the phone, often calling him a loser.

On the other hand, Alex could do no wrong in the eyes of The Don, and her stepfather probably felt he was getting a second chance at raising a son, which was why he doted on him. This made it all the more strange that Ron would want to help Alex do anything—unless it was to win favor with his father... or their mother.

Ron turned and kissed Abby's mom on the cheek and said, "When Alex is ready, I'll be waiting outside," and he left. Abby took that as her cue to head for her room so she could send a text to her dad begging him not to do anything that would land him in jail. Then she would sneak back into her stepdad's office to search for more clues. For someone her age, she sure had a lot on her plate—but someone had to be the adult in this house.

CHAPTER 24

THE DON WAS HIS USUAL "DR. JEKYLL AND MR. Hyde" self as he stepped out of his Bentley Continental and made his way into the country club, of which he was a founding member. When the valet asked if he wanted his already-gleaming car washed, he simply replied, "Piss off." However, when a longstanding member of the club (and a member of the board) approached, McCallister was all smiles.

"This is Andre, the boy I told you about the other day," the board member said to The Don. "He'll be part of our foursome."

"Andre, how are things at San Diego High?" Don asked, with a shake of the boy's hand.

"Uh, they're good. It's all good," he replied, nervous and not quite sure what to say to the richest man he'd ever met—and an old white man at that.

"You know, I went to San Diego High when I was a kid. Obviously, that was a long time ago."

"Yeah, that's what I heard. Plus, the gym is named after you, so…."

"Right you are, Andre. It's good to give back. Speaking of which, can I buy you lunch before we play? I hear the food is pretty good here," McCallister said with a wink, since he micromanaged the club to the point of picking out many of the menu items and naming them after famous mobsters.

"Sure," Andre replied.

"I hear you're the current class president, Andre. That's good. Where do you plan to go to college?"

"Well, I really don't know. I can't really afford to go to a university, so I'll probably just start at a community college and see what happens."

"That's fine. Good plan. But if money was no object, which school would you choose?"

Andre didn't hesitate. His dream school was Pepperdine University, and he said so.

"Great choice. Who knows? With your grades and extracurricular activities, you may end up getting a scholarship."

"That would be like a miracle, Mr. McCallister," Andre said as the small group made their way into the club.

In fact, Andre would end up getting a full ride, paid for by McCallister, but the kid would never know that. It was one of the many ways The Don secretly gave back. To date he had anonymously paid for over a dozen inner city kids to go to college who would have otherwise been unable to afford it. McCallister would have loved to publicize his "gifts for good grades" to the press, but he worried he would have people coming out of the woodwork asking him to pay their tuition, so he reluctantly kept this philanthropic gesture to himself.

As the large ornate doors shut behind The Don, Andre, and the board member, a yellow VW van pulled up to the valet stand.

"Are you a guest here, sir?" the valet asked as Thomas stepped out and towered over him. Even though some of the current and former Chargers came to the club to play golf and Thomas had the right physique, the valet could see he wasn't dressed for the occasion. His cargo shorts and aloha shirt were deemed inappropriate attire by the board, plus he didn't have any shoes… or clubs.

"I'm supposed to meet Don McCallister. Is he here yet?"

"You just missed him. I think I heard him say he was going to order lunch. Go through the doors and the dining room is to the right." The valet didn't get paid enough to even try to refuse entry to Thomas or call him out on his attire. Someone inside could do that. Plus, there was the hope of a good tip if this really was a former pro football player. But instead, Thomas just gave him a pat on the shoulder as he walked away.

"Sir, your car. I need the keys," the valet called out.

"Just leave it where it is. I'll be right back," Thomas replied without looking back.

"But it's right in front of the door."

"Exactly," Thomas said, as he left the valet standing there dumbfounded.

CHAPTER 25

WHILE RON AND ALEX WERE ON THEIR WAY TO a park to practice football, Ron received a text and read it while he drove. He screamed and slammed his hands on the steering wheel, scaring his stepbrother to the point of tears.

"Sorry, bro, but it looks like football training will have to wait. Something came up."

Ron swung a u-turn to take Alex back home. Alex sat in silence, afraid to say a word.

CHAPTER 26

"I DON'T KNOW WHAT HAPPENED. WHEN I pulled him out he looked like this."

"You mean, *dead,*" the other lab technician said as he pulled down his surgical mask and looked at the purple-colored man. There was no longer a need to hide his identity or pretend he was a doctor.

"So what do we do with him now?"

"Well we can't use him for testing, which is a shame. Depending on when he died, we may be able to harvest his organs and sell them on the black market," the lab tech said.

"What? I am not cutting someone up and selling off his body parts. That's messed up."

"Why not? Is it so different than what we are doing?"

"Do I really need to answer that? What we are doing is science. What you're suggesting is… I don't know what it is, but it's not what I signed up for."

"We need money, and you'd be surprised at how much people will pay for vital organs."

"How much?"

"An arm and a leg."

"Okay, that's not funny. Besides, neither of us have

enough experience to pull it off. Just because you were able to fence off the stuff we stole from the houses in our neighborhood, it doesn't mean you can find a buyer for a kidney or a spleen."

"First of all, people don't buy spleens. Secondly, I'm only messing with you. Neither of us has the training to remove anything more than a testicle."

"A testicle! You had to say that! That made the hair on my neck stand up and my body twitch—especially down there."

"At some point you're gonna have to get over your squeamishness about cutting people up because we're gonna need liver samples when we're done with the testing."

"I thought you said we were hiring someone with experience to do that?"

"It's not that easy. Think about it. We've kidnapped over a dozen people, held them against their will, subjected them to a drug study that is so new nobody knows what the side effects will be, and now we've accidentally killed someone."

"We still have that doctor lined up, plus his girlfriend is a nurse."

"Relax, it's all under control. We give the samples to the doctor and he'll do the rest, just like we planned."

"Really? When's the last time you saw him?"

"After he got us set up. His presence isn't as important until we get closer to the end."

"Doesn't it strike you as odd that to do something legitimate like start a pharmaceutical company we have to commit multiple felonies?"

"I guess when you say it like that it does seem kind of ironic. The way I look at it is, we're maturing. We can't continue doing petty crime while we wait for our parents to croak so we can inherit their money. For all we know they're already overextended and all that will be left is their debt. Plus, we can't kill them. We'd be the first ones the police would suspect."

"The boss may want to kill his parents, especially his dad, but I'm not going all Menendez brothers on my folks. So small crimes it is for now. Speaking of petty crime, how much money did the dead guy have in his wallet?"

"I don't know, I didn't check it yet," the tech said and passed the wallet to his partner.

"Well, whaddya know—for once, there actually is some cash. There's twenty, forty, sixty, eighty, one hundred dollars in here," the tech said as he rifled through the wallet. "Hey, get this… this guy's last name is Wiener. Wiener. Man, that's gotta suck."

The other "lab tech" just rolled his eyes at the double entendre.

CHAPTER 27

THOMAS QUICKLY SPOTTED THE DON HAVING lunch with an African-American teenager and two of his cronies wearing gaudy pink golf shirts. He also noted there was either a security guard or bodyguard standing near the table. Thomas walked right up to the man and put out his hand as if to shake it and head-butted the guard so hard he was unconscious before he hit the ground. It happened so fast most of the diners didn't even notice right away, but Don McCallister did—and he was afraid. He jumped up and started backing away from the table, spilling coffee on his ridiculous white golf pants.

"You know why I'm here," Thomas said as he moved closer to The Don.

"I don't know what you want, but you're not going to get it by hurting me."

"What makes you think I'm going to hurt you? You'll be dead so fast you won't feel a thing," Thomas said in such a menacing and convincing way that it made the other people at McCallister's table stand up and back away as well, especially Andre.

"Look, whatever you think it is I've done, let's talk about it and I'm sure we can find some sort of agreeable resolution. There's no need for violence."

"You stole my wife, my kids, my house, my money, and now the park. What do I have left to lose?"

"Now, wait just a minute. I didn't steal anything from you. You lost it. I was just there to step in—"

"Shut up, Don. What I want to know before I snap your neck is what you did with all the people at the park?"

"I don't know what you're talking about. What people? What park?"

"You know what I mean and you're going to tell me what I want to know."

Thomas moved so fast, not one person reacted as he lunged forward and grabbed McCallister by the neck and lifted him off the ground. Nobody nearby even had time to flinch, not that Thomas cared. This was his end game. He was going to kill the man who had ruined his life, and whatever happened after that didn't matter. He was so focused on what he was doing—and about to do—Thomas didn't immediately feel his cheap cell phone buzzing in his pocket. The only person who ever called or texted him was Abby, so it wasn't very often it buzzed. Besides, half the time the thing wasn't even charged or the bill paid.

"I know you have something planned for the park, and the only way to get your hands on the property is to get rid of the people living there. So what did you do, Don?"

The Don couldn't answer, with the vice-like grip of Big Mac's hand around his throat, so he tried to shake his head to indicate "I didn't do anything," but he was quickly beginning to lose consciousness.

"I need to know where my friends are, Don, and you're going to tell me," Thomas said before his phone buzzed again in his pocket. As he held The Don up with one hand, he used his other to reach in his pocket and pull out his phone.

"Hello?"

"Dad, where are you?"

"I can't talk, honey. I kinda have my hands full right now. Let me call you back when I'm done, okay?"

"Dad, tell me you aren't with Don."

"Okay, I won't tell you that."

"But you are, aren't you?"

"Yes, but I don't think he's feeling so good right at the moment."

"Dad, what did you do!?"

"We're just having a little chat, that's all, Honey." At this point, several people had quietly left the dining room to notify management and call the police. Those who remained were motionless, stunned that some big goon was manhandling one of the club's most valued members.

"I know you, Dad. How bad is it?"

"He's still alive, if that's what you mean."

"Don't do it. Ritchie and I have something to show you that will prove Don did it, or at least most likely did it. You don't have to hurt him. We can use the law—"

"Did you say you and *Ritchie*!?" Thomas interrupted. "You mean the reporter? You two have been talking? Stay away from him. He's a grown man."

"Okay, Dad, if you stop whatever it is you're doing to Don, I will stop talking to Ritchie. Do we have a deal?"

"Deal." Thomas threw Don to the carpet several feet away, like he was a third-string rookie safety. "The matter is now out of my hands. I want you and that reporter to meet me at our secret spot in thirty minutes." Thomas hung up and walked to McCallister, who was gasping for air and crawling to get away from the big man.

"I… I… didn't do anything wrong," Don said over his shoulder in a raspy voice.

"I don't care about your plans for the park. All I want to know is what you did with the people who lived there. The ones who are missing."

The Don was now butt down on the carpet, still trying to catch his breath. "What people? What people!?" he squeaked out.

"This isn't over. My daughter just saved your life… for now. If you don't bring back all of the people from the park by tomorrow, I will kill you. Do you understand?"

Don shook his head no.

Thomas leaned down a little closer, and shook his head in disbelief. "That's too bad, McCallister. I wanted to give you a chance to do the right thing for once in your life, but it looks like your life is going to come to a very violent end."

CHAPTER 28

"RITCHIE, MY DAD WANTS TO MEET WITH BOTH of us," Abby said over the phone.

"Really? Okay, when and where?"

"Do you know what the tide is?"

"What? The tide? Why?"

"My dad wants us to go to our secret meeting place, and it's only accessible at low tide."

"Hang on, let me check," Ritchie said and used an app on his phone to find out that the tide was indeed low. "It's actually a minus tide in an hour."

"Perfect. Look, you'd never find the place unless I show you. Meet me at Big Rock in ten minutes and I'll take you to the spot."

"Bird Rock?"

"No, *Big* Rock."

"Oh, right… the surf spot in La Jolla."

"Yeah. Meet me at the back entrance to the beach. I can lock my bike up there and we can drive the rest of the way together."

"Okay, I'll be there."

Ten minutes later Abby, waited on the sidewalk for the red Mustang to drive down Camino de la Costa. Ritchie stopped and Abby hopped in, not opening the door.

"Good one," Ritchie said with a smile.

"You're right, it is easier than opening the door."

"And way cooler, too. So, where is this secret spot?" Ritchie asked. It had certainly crossed his mind that Mr. MacDonald was plotting to kill him for spending time with his daughter, and this would be the place to do it… low tide or not.

"Just drive south on this road and I'll show you."

They sat in silence for the few minutes it took to get to the beach access sign hidden between two giant mansions overlooking the ocean.

"Park here, it's down that path," Abby said hopping out of the car, not waiting for Ritchie to follow.

"Slow down. We're early."

"I want to get down there and hide to make sure nobody followed us or my dad."

"Nobody followed us, that's for sure. Look around, there's nobody here." Ritchie gestured with both arms open toward the absence of anyone around them.

Abby led her partner-in-crime-solving down a narrow trail that continued to a small cove sheltered by the cliffs and the massive homes perched on them.

"Wow! This is amazing," he said. "It's like a postcard or something. Look at the water. You can see the reef and the fish. It's so blue."

"I know. My dad and I would meet here after the divorce because it's the one place nobody but us knew about."

"How did your dad find it?"

"I guess when he was a kid he would come down

here and paddle out to surf the wave that breaks out there," Abby pointed to a spot off shore. "Nobody surfs it because it's almost impossible to get to and the wave is really dangerous. It breaks in super shallow water and most of the waves close out, but my dad is fearless."

"Do you know why your dad wants to meet here?"

"No. But I think he may be in trouble."

Abby filled Ritchie in on the call to her father and her fear of what he may have done to Don.

"Don't you think it's a little strange that he forbid you from seeing me and then asked me to meet him here? He could be setting me up," Ritchie said with nervousness in his voice.

"I thought the same thing, but I wouldn't worry about it. As long as I'm here, you're safe."

"And if you're not here, then what?"

"Run."

Thomas was so stealthy that Abby and Ritchie didn't notice him sneak up on them as they sat on the sand with several feet of space between them.

"Ah, you're both here," Thomas said as he jumped down from the cliff and landed in the sand with a thud.

Ritchie practically lost his breath in a gasp at the big man's sudden appearance. "Holy mother of God! You nearly scared the—" He caught his language before it came out in front of Abby. "You nearly scared me to death." He took and let out a deep breath, as Abby cracked a bit of a smile.

"Oh, I forgot to tell you," she said, "my dad has a secret passage to get to our secret spot."

"Were you two followed?" Thomas asked.

"No. Were you?" Abby asked back.

Thomas raised an eyebrow to silently signal *Really?* to her.

"Dad, what did you do to Don?"

"Don't worry about it. Tell me what you know about the park."

Ritchie immediately spoke up. "I know you don't like me spending time with Abby. But just for the record, I am only helping Abby help *you*. That's it. You've gotta believe me."

"Relax, Ritchie. I believe you and I appreciate your help. Now tell me what you found out about our old friend, Don McCallister."

The two explained what they had learned from Don's home office and Ritchie's research and interview with Jeff Wiener. Thomas told the two of them what he'd surmised, leaving out his recent violent visit to the country club.

"So what do you conclude from what we now know, Ritchie?" Thomas asked.

"Well, I think we all agree the one person who has the most to gain from getting people out of the park is McCallister," Ritchie replied. "But what bothers me is why he would go to such extremes when he could just use his political pull and legal team to do the dirty work. Making people disappear seems drastic, unless there is some deadline or reason or something we don't know about."

"You know, I didn't think of that. It's a good point and something you should look into," Thomas said to

Ritchie in a surprisingly warm way.

"What about me, Dad?"

"Tell me your theory, Honey."

"I agree with Ritchie. There is more going on here than we are seeing. You hate Don, and who can blame you? So it's possible you want to put this all on him because that would be the perfect way to get back at him—but maybe you aren't seeing things in an objective way. What if we looked at it from another angle?"

"Fair enough. So who else would benefit by making people vanish and force the City to come in and take back the park?"

The three looked at each other, but no one had an answer.

"Dad, I took pictures of some of the plans I found for the park in Don's desk drawer, but they were too hard to read so I went back in and stole them."

Ritchie looked at Abby and smiled, as did her dad.

"Good work, Abby. Ritchie, while you're trying to find out if there's a pressing permit problem or some other reason why this is happening now, maybe you can also talk to the staff for the mayor and a council member or two to see if there's some political possibility to explain what's going on. Abby, do you have a friend you can stay with for couple of days?"

"Why can't I come with you, Dad?"

"That would not be a good idea, trust me."

"What are you going to do?" she asked, worry evident in her voice.

"I, uh, I have to lay low for a while. Since I have some experience with blueprints, I'll review the plans.

Here's my new number. I bought a burner phone and ditched my old one because I don't want anyone tracking my whereabouts."

"Which will be...?" Abby asked hopefully.

"The less you know, the better," Thomas replied, as he left the same way he came, but this time with the plans under his arm.

CHAPTER 29

"SMITTY, THIS IS DON. I NEED A FAVOR," DON MC Callister said as he left a voicemail for his good friend, the sheriff.

The sheriff called back immediately, which was the norm since it was Don who filled his election and re-election war chest over the years with both ethical and unethical contributions. Don truly believed his buddy was the right man for the job, plus it had paid off ten times over having a person high up in law enforcement—especially with a son that was constantly getting in trouble.

"What can I do for you, buddy?" the sheriff asked.

"Is it safe to talk on the phone?"

"Uh-oh, this can't be good. Nobody is monitoring my phone, how about you?"

"I don't know. But it would be best if there is no recording of what I want to tell you."

"Let's meet at our usual spot in, say, thirty minutes," the sheriff suggested.

That was the kind of respect The Don demanded, the drop-everything-and-see-to-his-needs kind, so Sheriff Smith agreed and left to drive up the hill to a lookout spot in La Jolla that was known only to the most local of locals.

It was in an area called Munchkinville, where rumor had it that several little people who had made money in movies in the fifties and sixties bought lots hidden in the hills and built custom homes that were sized down to accommodate them. The myth lived on, in part, because the area included a tiny one-lane bridge and a few single-story homes with small doors and low windows.

There was a path next to one of these homes that led to a piece of prime property with a stunning view of the coast. To Don's dismay, it was owned by the city. All that was on the point was a single bench in the dirt. Over the years Don had tried to acquire the land, but it wasn't for sale. Since it was almost impossible to find and access was limited, McCallister came here to be alone and think or to meet with his key people when he wanted to have a confidential conversation.

"So, what is so important we had to meet? Is Ron in trouble again?" Sheriff Smith asked as he sat down on the bench.

"Probably, but that's not why I want to talk to you. It's about MacDonald."

"Let it go, buddy. Haven't you done enough to the guy already?"

"In a word, no. He's like a cockroach; he just won't die. Plus, he assaulted me."

"When?"

"Today, at the club."

"Are you hurt?"

"That's not the point. He humiliated me in front of everyone. That's the last straw. I want him dead."

"We are speaking metaphorically here, right?'

"No, I mean I want him d-e-a-d, dead. Not breathing. Gone from this earth. And I want it done in a way that is shameful so everyone thinks he's a monster or a pervert or a thief."

"I can't believe we're having this conversation, Don. You'd be the first person people would point to as a prime suspect."

"Not if I have an airtight alibi that involved over a hundred people and a sitting Sheriff."

Sheriff Smith sighed and shook his head. "Don, I don't want to get involved in a murder, even if it's just as an alibi witness. This could backfire in a big way if something goes wrong. Besides, killing your wife's ex was never part of the plan."

"I want to take everything he has and everything he's ever gonna have."

"That sounds like a line from a movie."

"It is—it's from a Clint Eastwood flick. Look, I tried it your way and the guy is still a menace and interfering with my plans."

"Just for the sake of stopping you from doing something you'll regret, tell me what you're thinking."

CHAPTER 30

WHEN THE EFFECTS OF THE DRUGS WORE OFF, Shaggy first fought the panic of being strapped down in a dark coffin-like tomb, and then he listened. Being kept in the dark and restrained, hearing was the only one of his senses he could use. From time to time he would hear a familiar voice cry out. At first he couldn't place the person. Then, one by one, he started to recognize the sounds of a few he knew—Rusty Nails, Pumpkin Head, Whitey, and finally, Teen Wolf. They were all people from the park. With time to think, Shaggy figured out what was happening. Someone was using homeless people like himself to test some sort of drug.

Once they had inserted the needle in his arm, they rarely checked on him. Since he wasn't being fed and the only water he was allowed came from a water bottle taped to the top of his tomb with a tube that hung down, he didn't have to go to the bathroom much, but when he did he just peed on himself. Shaggy felt like a prisoner of war, but his treatment and conditions were much worse. This study couldn't possibly be legal, and professionals certainly weren't conducting it.

Sometimes when he was lucid, Shaggy would catch part of a conversation between the lab technicians and they sounded like amateurs—which made this all the more scary. These weren't medical professionals, so if something went wrong what could they do? Maybe that could work to his advantage, though. If he started screaming like he was in great pain, maybe they would pull him out and he could escape.

The problem with this, Shaggy surmised, was three-fold. One, he was strapped down so they would have to first remove his restraints. Two, if he did manage to get free, he was too weak to walk—or fight. Three, they might just kill him instead of trying to help him. As slim as his chances were, not doing anything at all was far more grim—and depressing. Scheming was keeping him from total panic and despair.

So Shaggy made up his mind. He would pretend to lose it and see what happened. It couldn't get any worse, so he had little to lose. Shaggy began to scream and moan as if he were dying—which wasn't much of a stretch because he was, in fact, dying a slow death. He kept up the charade for a few minutes but nothing happened, so he ratcheted it up until he heard muffled voices nearby. This is it; this is his chance to escape. He would be ready.

Instead, he felt the familiar rush of the drug in his veins and within a few minutes he blacked out again.

CHAPTER 31

WHEN RITCHIE DROPPED ABBY OFF BACK AT BIG Rock Beach where her bike was locked up, he told her to be careful, and she took what he said to heart as she rode away. Out of the corner of her eye she spotted a white van parked across the street with two guys sitting in it trying to look inconspicuous, which made them all the more conspicuous. Abby pretended not to notice them as she peddled toward home.

Sure enough, the van pulled out from the curb, made a U-turn and began following her. She snuck a glance back as she turned left down Palomar Street and then made a quick right on Neptune Place. The beach was packed with people, which eased her fears. She wouldn't take her usual route home through the back streets of Bird Rock because that would leave her exposed and vulnerable. So she rode on past Windansea Beach and carefully pulled the phone out of her pocket and pretended to make a call, but what she was really doing was trying to get a few quick pics of the van and possibly the license plate. She snapped over a dozen different shots hoping at least one of them captured the front of the van.

When Abby rounded the corner just after Little

Point, she zipped into a driveway that doubled as a beach access for those in the know. She didn't dare look back and tip off the people in the van that she was on to them. She walked her bike down to the sand and sat on a rock to scroll through the pictures on her phone. In the glare of the summer sun it was hard to see, but she could tell right away—although her idea was a good one in theory, in reality most of the pictures were either blurry or missed the mark.

One picture, however, held some promise. The van was visible, but the front license plate had been removed. What she could determine was the make and model. Also, the people sitting in the front seat looked vaguely familiar, but Abby wasn't sure where she might have seen them before. It wasn't much to go on, but it was a start.

CHAPTER 32

IN HIS PLAYING DAYS, THOMAS LIKED TO KEEP his hair long and his beard unruly. It made him look threatening, and on the football field he *was* a scary guy. When he retired from the NFL and started his construction company, he cut his hair and trimmed his beard because he dealt with a lot of female customers (and their husbands) who would be intimidated by a tall, muscular, hairy man who looked like he'd just stepped out of the woods rather than completed an illustrious football career.

When his wife left him, Thomas started drinking heavily and let himself go. Although he could polish off a big bottle of tequila in under an hour, he lost his appetite and actually lost weight. Once he began living in his van, personal hygiene was not a priority. So, people who knew him from his time with the Chargers, or more recently when he became homeless, recognized him by his long scraggly hair and Duck Dynasty-like beard. Now that he needed to lay low, he decided it was time to disguise himself by getting rid of these identifying features.

It was not an easy decision to carry out, but he did it. Thomas started with a pair of scissors and trimmed his beard down to size and then shaved it off. When he looked in the mirror he didn't even recognize himself. Then he hacked off most of his hair, but it looked ridiculous—so he contemplated shaving his head, but decided against it. He decided instead to splurge and spend the $7.00 to get a proper haircut at a barbershop on Girard Avenue in La Jolla that had been there since the 1950s.

It was worth it when he walked out and saw his reflection in the window of Warwick's Book Store—he hardly recognized the clean-cut and clean-shaven man staring back at him. Now he just had to find a way to get around in something other than in his well-known and hard-to-miss van. It was time to call in a favor.

Despite the bad publicity surrounding his downfall and divorce, Thomas's fellow offensive linemen, those he went to battle with on the weekends for ten years, still stood by his side. The most important person on an offensive line, other than maybe the blind-side tackle, is the center. He is the signal-caller, puts every play into motion, and lines up directly next to the guard—Big Mac's former position.

Since Thomas was drafted quickly in the first round, there was little doubt he would start—plus, in 1983 it was rare to find a lineman who weighed over 300 pounds and could move like he could. So the Chargers kept veteran center Doug Mack on for one last season to help the rookie get through his first year in the league without hurting the team or anyone else.

The starting quarterback, Dan Fouts, called his two best linemen "Big Mac" and "Little Mack" because

Thomas was taller and outweighed the older and smaller center by almost 60 pounds. Despite their age differences, the two became fast friends and remained so even after Little Mack retired at the end of the season. Thomas was a throwback, and his old-school style of play, lunch-pail mentality, and work ethic when it came to preparing for a game were beyond his years. This endeared him to the veterans—and they told him so—and encouraged Thomas to be a good example for the other linemen coming into the league. What he learned about football and life from his mentor, Big Mac vowed to pass on to younger players who were drafted after him.

The following season, the Chargers drafted a rookie center to replace Little Mack and promoted two other backups to fill out the starting line. They were all around the same age and they all had the same nasty disposition on the field—except for the new center, Max Webster.

Max Webster didn't have a nickname because he didn't really need one. He was easily the smartest person on the team (and maybe in all of football), so calling him Webster—short for *Webster's Dictionary*—was fitting. It was soon shortened to just "Web," but it didn't matter because everyone respected him for his mastery of the playbook and knowledge of the game—even as a rookie.

The problem was, he was an anomaly, being a massive man who loved to play not just football but chess, Scrabble, and other heady games as well. He kept to himself when he first joined the team, but Big Mac decided to help the rookie along even though Big Mac was only in the second year of his own career. The two roomed together in training camp and would stay up late talking about anything and everything—certainly football, but mostly about life. Thomas learned a lot from his new friend off the field and Webster benefitted from Big Mac's tutelage on the field.

It was rare for an offensive line to remain intact for very long due to injuries, trades, and free agency. Yet, Thomas and several other linemen played together for several years. He and Max Webster were together for eleven of the twelve years MacDonald played, including their one and only Super Bowl appearance. That year, the players earned extra money from winning two playoff games and making it to the big game—which they unfortunately lost, and badly, to the 49ers. Thomas and Max decided to spend some of that Super Bowl money on two Harley Davidson Softails, which they often took on long drives to the desert and mountains outside of San Diego.

When Thomas knew he was going to lose everything in his divorce, he asked his friend and teammate to hide a few of his prized possessions—his Super Bowl ring and other memorabilia he feared his wife would sell or destroy. He also asked Max to keep his Harley hidden in his garage. Thankfully, his wife didn't remember he had it when she went after all of his assets. Hopefully, it was still sitting there all these years later.

"Max, howya doin'?" Thomas asked as his former teammate opened the door at his home.

"I wouldn't recognize you if I didn't hear your van coming down the street and then see it pull into my driveway. I see you finally cleaned yourself up."

"You're looking good, Web. Lost some weight?"

"Do I look like I lost weight?"

"Well, no, but it seemed like the right thing to say." They both chuckled.

"I've been busy with my business so I don't have time to go to the gym. How do you stay so slim?"

"Try being homeless for two years and see how much weight you lose."

"Sorry. I know, I know. Come in, come in."

"You been in touch with any of the guys?" Thomas asked as he filled the doorway on his way through.

"Not really. I mean, I kind of lost touch with everyone after you, uh, well, you know, your life got turned upside down. I went to Junior's funeral and saw some of the guys, but when you count his death, that's eight players from our Super Bowl team who are dead before the age of 45."

"Wait, eight? Who?"

"You know about Griggsy crashing his car, and Culver was in a plane that went down in the Everglades, right?"

"Yeah. I was better at keeping in touch with teammates back then. Didn't Doug Miller get struck by lightning when he was camping a while back?" Thomas asked, but he knew the answer already.

"Yep… died in 1998. That's three. You know about Whitley?" Max asked.

"Your backup. No, what happened to him?"

"It sounded like it was an overdose. It happened right after Mims had a heart attack. Did you know that

Mims weighed over 400 pounds when he died? Same with Shawn Lee," Max announced.

"Oh, man," Thomas said, surprised.

"And Junior became the eighth."

"Yeah, I heard. I'm sure I'm high on everyone's list to go next. Did I hear that Junior shot himself in the stomach to leave his brain intact to test for CTE?"

"It looks that way. Wait, we forgot about Lew. He was the seventh to die. Another heart attack."

"I helped him with the buildout on Sweet Lew's BBQ restaurant before he died. The place was right around the corner from my house and I used to take the family there once a week. Now that I think back on it, I took the kids with me to see Lew, but I had no idea where my ex was—now I do, though."

"How are Abby and Alex?" Max said, trying to change the subject. He was never a big fan of Madison, Thomas' ex-wife.

"Abby's great. I don't see Alex much."

"Sorry about that."

"Are you married, Web?"

"Nope. Just to my work."

"You still in the video game business?"

"Yup. Why, you need a job?"

"Probably, but that's not why I'm here," Thomas said. "I was wondering if you still have my bike in the garage?"

"Of course. It's right where you left it. I start it up from time to time and keep the battery on a charger."

"You're the best, Web. Do you mind if I borrow a helmet and park my van in your garage for a little while?"

"Are you planning to still live in your van?"

"Ya know, I guess I didn't think that through. Do you mind?"

"Not at all, but you're certainly welcome to the couch."

"Umm..." Thomas was a stubbornly independent person, but he didn't want to seem ungrateful. "That's cool of you, Web, but I kinda need my space at the moment. Got a lotta stuff on my mind. I hope you understand."

"Sure. Whatever works for you. If you change your mind, just let me know," Max said as he put his arm around his old friend and led him to the garage of his suburban home.

CHAPTER 33

"RITCHIE, WHERE ARE YOU?" JULIE, HIS EDITOR, whispered into the phone.

"Why are you whispering?" Ritchie replied, instinctively whispering as well even though he was alone in his car.

"There are two sheriff's deputies going through the things on your desk as we speak."

"Good luck with that."

"This is serious, Ritchie."

"I'm serious. My desk is a mess. I only use it to store stuff I don't need—which is just about everything."

"You're not listening to me—this isn't a joke."

"I think it is," he said with a touch of indignation. "Just because I wrote an article exposing the homeless problem in San Diego and how many of these people are suddenly nowhere to be found, now the powers-that-be want to see my notes? What can they do, force me to reveal my source? I can't even get hold of him. So—"

"Ritchie, I overheard them say something about you and a twelve-year-old girl." Her voice was now a heightened hushed tone, trying to convey the seriousness to Ritchie while not alerting the deputies to her call.

"What!? Abby? No, no, no. It's not what you think."

"So you know this girl? Tell me you didn't do this."

"Julie, come on. You know me."

"That's the problem."

"I didn't touch her. I didn't do anything."

"But you obviously know what this is about?"

"I know *who* this is about. But I don't know what's going on. Let's just call her a source right now."

"Did you take her anywhere in your car, Ritchie?"

"How would they know that??" he asked.

"I don't know. Maybe they were watching you. So did you?"

"Uh, well, yeah… I gave her a ride home once, but that's it. Oh, and I drove her like a quarter-mile to a meeting with her dad earlier today."

"Ritchie, seriously. You're in trouble, *again*."

"What? I didn't *do* anything."

"So why do they think you did?" Julie pleaded. She glanced into the room where Ritchie's desk was, to be sure they were still preoccupied with it.

"I don't know. All Abby—the girl—and I did was discuss the story about the homeless park where her dad lives. Did I mention she's the daughter of Thomas MacDonald, formerly of the Chargers, and the step-daughter of Don McCallister, the devil… I mean, the developer? Her dad is totally fine with it. He likes me… I think. It's hard to tell. I only met the stepfather one time at his front door, and he seemed like a real jerk. And besides—"

"Got it," Julie said, cutting him off because he was starting to ramble. "And that explains it."

"It does?" Ritchie replied.

"Ritchie, wake up. Don McCallister is good friends with the sheriff and he hates Thomas, who is his wife's ex—who also just so happens to live at the park. He's trying to set you up and, as sick as this sounds, he's using his own stepdaughter to do it.

"Aw, man. I didn't see that coming."

"Right. So be careful, okay?"

"'Careful' is my middle name," Ritchie said.

"Yeah, but 'Careless' is your first and last name," Julie reminded him.

"Ouch."

"The truth hurts. Just watch yourself. Some powerful people are in play here," Julie said before she covered the phone with her hand. "The sheriffs say they found something. I gotta go. Remember what I said."

"Julie, can you meet me in my 'office' tonight for a drink?" Ritchie asked, emphasizing the word *office* so Julie would know he meant to meet him at Tug's Tavern across the street.

"Your office? Oh, your *office*. I'll see what I can do."

"I'll be in the back by the dartboard at seven o'clock," and he hung up.

CHAPTER 34

THOMAS SAT IN THE SALON OF HIS OLD BOAT, even though he had long ago sold the beloved 1968 Luhrs cabin cruiser when his fortunes turned and he needed the money. Fortunately, the new owner hadn't changed the locks and Thomas still had the key. The vintage vessel was renamed, and the buyer bought all kinds of new things to improve the already-beautiful boat, but all of the custom woodwork Thomas had crafted was still intact—but not nearly as meticulously maintained. The thirty-two-foot boat was still stored in the same slip. He'd parked his motorcycle in a far corner of the marina's lot and walked the long way around to B Dock to avoid being seen by the dockmaster, who knew him well, or anyone else who might recognize him. Mission accomplished. Thomas knew that June was the beginning of the season for those who lived in Arizona during the winter but came to San Diego to escape the Arizona heat and enjoy their boats for the summer. The new owners would be back sometime this month, but he needed somewhere quiet and familiar to think, so he came aboard for the first time in a long while.

Thomas turned the lights on, spread the stolen blueprints out on the small table in the cozy cabin, and began studying them to see exactly what the developer had in mind for the park. Right away Thomas knew something was wrong. These plans had to be fakes. There was no way what he was looking at could be right. He double- and triple-checked everything again and couldn't believe what he was seeing. It couldn't be—but there it was in black and white (or blue and gray since these were actually blueprints). Thomas was stunned and needed a drink, so he raided the liquor cabinet, found a bottle of Don Julio, and poured some into a coffee cup.

"You're gonna need another cup," said a voice from behind him that caused Thomas to jump. Peering in through a porthole was Les Davis, the dockmaster. "I know better than to sneak up on you from behind. Permission to come aboard?"

"Since it's not my boat anymore, the answer is yes," Thomas said and rose to greet his old friend.

"It's okay, the owner never comes around. You can tell because he'd kept this boat in perfect condition before he got sick. Paul developed Parkinson's Disease, and a boat is no place for a person with that condition. He hasn't been around in a while."

"I'm sorry to hear that. How are you doing? How's the gang?"

Before Les Davis could answer there was a rap on the hull. "Who's in there?"

"Hi, Christie. It's me and Thomas MacDonald," Les answered.

"Thomas is here?" Christie said with excitement. "Mind if me and Trevor come aboard?"

"Long time, no see," Trevor chimed in. The husband

and wife had met at the marina years earlier and now their boats were slipped side by side. She had been an Olympic volleyball player and Trevor James played right field for the Padres *before* Tony Gwynn took over. He's the guy nobody can remember.

"You're all welcome to come aboard," Thomas said and gave each a hug as they boarded his old boat. It was just like old times, and Thomas felt a warmth he hadn't felt in quite some time.

"Wow, you're all… clean," Christie said to the now-beardless and short-haired MacDonald.

"Believe it or not, this is my incognito look," Thomas told them all.

"We heard what happened to you from Ann Marie," Trevor said.

"Yeah, she would come around to the park and bring me meals from the restaurant. Without her help I don't know what I would have done," Thomas explained. Ann Marie was a waitress at the Baja Grill where all the boaters went for happy hour since it was conveniently located next to the marina. Anyone who spent time at the Island Marina became part of the family, and the people now lounging in his old boat were some of his favorites. Ann Marie had said she couldn't watch him destroy his life, so she stopped coming around the homeless camp over a year earlier. "How is Ann Marie? How's her son?"

Les Davis jumped in: "She's doing really well, and her boy just graduated from high school this month. How are your kids?"

"Don't ask."

"I just did," Les shot back, still as snarky as he ever was. But he didn't know the magnitude of his question.

"I don't want to talk about it. Let's just have a drink," Thomas said as he got up to find more cups and poured everyone a shot.

"A toast," Les said, "To the good old days of the Island Marina!"

After Thomas gulped his tequila down, he asked, "How are things around here?"

"Not good," Les answered, his toast tone suddenly more somber. "After that developer guy bought the marina last year he started making changes, and one of those changes was me. He fired me, Thomas," the now-former dockmaster said, clearly upset.

"What? You helped build this place."

"I know. I was only here tonight to come and get some of my things from the office when I saw the light on in your boat." Thomas liked it being called his boat. "As far as I'm concerned, nothing good will come of McCallister owning this place. And that's not just sour grapes." Thomas's eyes widened.

"*Don McCallister*?"

"You didn't know?" Trevor asked. Thomas shook his head, his mind turning far more than the others could possibly tell.

"Yep. Over a year ago," Christie added. "He bought the marina and all the buildings around it. I hear he's planning to level everything and put up a big hotel."

"I hate to ask," Trevor started hesitantly, "but isn't McCallister the guy who...?" He couldn't quite get the words out of his mouth, but he didn't need to.

"One and the same," Thomas plainly answered. "Speaking of that despicable excuse for a human being, I'm looking at some plans for another development he has in the works. Take a look and tell me what you think."

After each person looked at the plans, they were left scratching their heads at what they saw. Considering what The Don planned to do to their beloved marina, this didn't make any sense.

CHAPTER 35

"WHAT DID I TELL YOU ABOUT COMING TO THIS house?" Don screamed at his son over the phone.

"Dad, I was helping Alex with football."

"Yeah, and how did that go?"

"Something came up. Something important."

"You scared the kid half to death."

"Aw, come on, Dad. All I did was get a little mad for a minute."

"That's not what I heard. Alex said you had a major meltdown. Are you taking your meds? Are you?"

"Dad, it wasn't a big deal. It's fine."

"It's not fine unless I say it's fine, and I say it's not fine. Alex shouldn't have to witness one of your episodes. He's a normal kid."

"Dad, I'm normal."

"You think I don't know what you did when you were a kid? You think I don't know what you did with your buddies, the Bird Rock Bozos?"

"It's the Bird Rock Band of Brothers, Dad."

"Whatever. You were a bully then and you're a bully now. Stay away from Alex, stay away from my wife, and most of all, stay away from me."

"What about Abby?"

"What's wrong with you? Nobody in this house wants you around. Got it?"

"But Dad, I'm working on something really big... Dad? Dad?"

CHAPTER 36

ABBY SAT IN HER ROOM AFTER HER MOM HAD grounded her "for life." Somehow her mom knew everything—she knew Abby was still in touch with her father, secretly meeting with a reporter, and sneaking into her stepfather's office.

How her mom knew about breaking into The Don's office was easy. Abby was just caught red-handed, taking pictures of documents with her phone. Once her mom confiscated her phone she found a text or two to her dad. Abby had been trying to reach her father earlier in the day and hadn't yet wiped her phone clean, a habit she formed for just this reason—in case someone got hold of her phone. But how did her mom know she was working with Ritchie? It didn't make sense. She was very careful to cover her tracks and keep the partnership a secret. Then it hit her… the white van.

Her mom was having her followed. That's why the van was waiting for her where she left her bike by the beach. *Oh man,* she thought, *did Mom put a tracking device on my bike? Were they using the GPS to find and follow me?* She looked down at her shoes. *Could there be a chip in the sole of my Toms?* She quickly kicked them off and into a pile of dirty clothes in the corner. *Am I totally losing it and getting paranoid?*

All she had were questions, but as any good reporter would do, she would seek the truth and follow the answers wherever they led.

CHAPTER 37

"WHERE IS SHE?" DON ASKED HIS WIFE AS SHE sunned herself in her favorite lounge chair next to their backyard pool. Don didn't like the sun, didn't like to swim, and didn't like the way Madison spent her days drinking alone out back—but the benefits of having a trophy wife kept his complaints in check.

"Abby is locked in her room, just like you asked," Madison replied.

"Did you get her phone?" Don wanted to know.

"Yes, and her laptop. What is this all about?"

"It's about your ex."

"Big surprise. What did he do now?" she slurred.

"That's not important. What's important is that we make him pay."

"And how does keeping Abby in her room make that happen?" Madison wanted to know.

"We know the two of them have a special relationship. The only way to get to him is through her. I mean, we took away everything that ever meant anything to him, and he's still in our lives. He's like a cockroach that can't be killed. The only way to squash him once and for all is to knock him off—but that won't work because we'd be the first people they'd suspect."

"Unless it was an accident," Madison said while stirring her umpteenth drink of the day.

"We've already tried that, twice, and it didn't work. No, we need to drive him back to drinking *himself* to death, and cutting off any contact with Abby could do it," Don said, rubbing his neck where it was still red and sore from Big Mac's assault on him at the club.

"Honey, that could take weeks, months, years even. I want him gone now. Think about it. How many people from his football team have died under strange circumstances?" It was the first time she'd said something that resembled deep thinking in quite some time.

"I don't know, how many?" Don truly didn't know the answer.

"A lot. Plus, he could have that CTE thing all the NFL widows and wives are complaining about. I tried to get in on that lawsuit against the league, but since Thomas and I are divorced, I don't get a dime of the $765-million-dollar settlement. Nothing. But, I still have a life insurance policy on him and if he dies a natural death—like drowning or getting hit by a car—I get $1.5 million."

"Don't you mean *we* get $1.5 million?" Don asked with a perturbed tone.

"No, that money is mine. You already have yours and I want mine to do with what I want," Madison stated.

Don steered the conversation back to Abby. "Just keep Abby in her room and out of sight. I have another reason for her to be unaccounted for and it involves that reporter from that local rag," Don said as he rose to leave.

"What does the reporter have to do with anything?"

"Trust me, the less you know, the better. Let's just say it's all part of the plan."

"What plan?" Madison asked.

"What did I just say? Leave it to me. The reporter is going down and that's that. All I need you to do is keep Abby locked up. Is that too much to ask?" Don said as he stormed off.

Madison had already been wondering what she would get if her new husband died a sudden death, too. The prenup he forced her to sign left her with too small an amount of money (in her mind), but Madison wanted to be wealthy without having to be married to a man like Don McCallister. Don had a secret plan and so did she. With his son's help, she could kill two birds with one stone... so to speak.

CHAPTER 38

"RON, IT'S MADISON."

"Oh hi, *Mom*."

"What did I say about calling me that?" Madison said, regretting her partnership with him.

"Sorry, I'm just trying to be funny."

"Well you're not, so stop trying. I need a favor."

"Well, I need a little favor, too—if you know what I mean."

Madison ignored Ron's raunchy request and quickly said, "Something came up. I need you to do something for me, then maybe I'll do something for you."

"That special thing."

"Fine, I'll do that if you do what I tell you to do," Madison said as she walked around the pool to an area near the waterfall, just in case anyone could overhear her, like Don.

"I'm listening," Ron said.

Madison laid out her plan in simple terms since Ron wasn't the sharpest tool in the shed. But he could be a cold-hearted and dangerous tool, and for this little project he would have to be.

CHAPTER 39

RITCHIE'S PLAN TO QUESTION A STAFF MEMBER in the mayor's office or a few people he knew who were political insiders went out the window when he learned he was being sought by law enforcement. So instead of going to them he would let them come to him. Ritchie set up shop on a corner stool at the far end of the bar in Hobson's, an establishment across the street from city hall. After a long day of wheeling and dealing, the policy-makers, players, and the people behind the players came here to be seen and socialize with other politically ambitious folks. The food and eclectic drinks were expensive, but fortunately a number of lobbyists were also conveniently there to pick up a tab or two. From time to time the heavy-hitters would try to win influence by buying rounds for the house. More often, though, they met in dark corners of the establishment to pass a fat envelope of cash to a crooked politician or a staffer on the take.

Ritchie ordered another draft beer and watched as people began filling up the place right on schedule—just after five o'clock. The woman he was hoping to see walked in the door. Having attended every community meeting for the beach area, this ambitious aide would always speak on behalf of the councilman she worked for and, coincidently, whose district the homeless park was in. As a reporter, Ritchie interviewed her frequently on the record and got a lot of good tidbits off the record, too. Ritchie also knew her from the neighborhood. They were on the same softball team on Saturdays at Santa Clara Point and they both liked to play beach volleyball in South Mission Beach on Sundays.

"Suzy, over here," Ritchie said as he waved her over to his end of the busy bar. Suzy had an athletic look about her. She kept her dark hair short, barely wore any makeup, and preferred slacks to dresses. She looked almost exactly the same on the weekends, but instead of a pants suit she wore a bathing suit with athletic shorts.

"Hey, Ritchie, what are you doing downtown? I don't think I've ever seen you anywhere but at the beach."

"Trust me, I'd rather be at the beach right now, but I need to talk to you about something important."

"Okay, so talk," Suzy said.

"What do you know about the plans to push people out of the park on Mariner's Beach?"

"It's funny you would ask me about that because I spent the better part of today working on our position on this project."

"And...?"

"Ritchie, is this for an article, or are you just asking me as a concerned citizen?"

"I, uh, both I guess. I don't know. A lot of stuff is going down that doesn't make sense. For instance, why is the City all of a sudden evicting the residents from their homes?"

"First of all, I would hardly call them residents, and when you refer to their homes do you mean the cars they're living in? I don't want to come across as heartless, but the people who have been lucky enough to have access to this area over the years had to know this was coming. Plans for that land have been in the works for decades, but nothing happened because nobody wanted to displace people with nowhere else to go."

"So, what's changed?"

"A plan has come along that looks promising for the City."

"Are we talking about Don McCallister?"

"We are. Have you seen the proposal?" Suzy asked.

"No, but I know someone who has. So you're saying this is a good deal for the City?"

"That's what I'm saying. It's a win for the homeless, the public, and the political fallout will be minimal."

"So it's happening."

"Yup."

"When?"

"I'd say by next week we'll be ready to make an official announcement."

"Can I quote you on that?"

"On what? All I said is we will make an announcement next week. But Ritchie, you're asking the *wrong* questions."

"I am? What *should* I be asking?"

"How did the developer win the bid when a dozen different proposals were rejected?" she told him.

"Okay, I'm asking that question then."

"I wish I had the answer, but I don't. I, for one, would like to know how McCallister suddenly got his plans approved without so much as a whisper in the press about the process, or lack of process I should say."

Greg, the longtime bartender, came over to say hello and take their order. "The usual, Suzy? How about you, Ritchie? Another beer?"

"How do you know my name?" Ritchie asked.

"It's my business to know my customers' names."

"I'm impressed. Yeah, I'll have another beer, and put Suzy's drink on my tab."

"Too late. The man at the other end of the bar is picking up your tab."

The two looked to their right and recognized the generous patron right away. That's when Ritchie prepared to bolt for the back door, but the man held up his hands in surrender as he walked over.

"Ritchie, I'm not here to arrest you if that's what you're worried about," Sheriff Smith said. "I'm pretty sure you aren't the pervert you've been made out to be."

"You're only pretty sure? Pretty sure!?" Ritchie said in a high, nervous voice.

"Okay, I'm sure. Look, you made an enemy in someone I know really well and who I owe a few favors to. So when he made the accusations, I did a little investigating and you came up clean—but I still had a couple of my deputies go to your office to send a message from my friend. You were never going to be arrested or charged with anything and there is no paperwork on any of this. Now, before you think about taking this inside information and running back to write a story about it, I highly discourage that idea. Let's just say I'm sorry about the whole thing—and I don't often say I'm sorry, so let's just forget it. Deal?"

Ritchie just stared at the sheriff, not sure what to say and not sure he just heard what he thought he did. If only he had the recorder on his iPhone going.

"Hey, Ritchie, you're not going to cause me any problems, are you?" the sheriff asked to break the silence.

"Uh, no, Sheriff, of course not. So just to be clear, I don't have to worry about being picked up for questioning?"

"That's right."

"But how do I clear my good name? Specifically with my boss?"

"Like I said, don't push it. Enjoy your beer, lay low, and this whole thing will blow over soon and you can go back to writing about whatever you want."

"Like the Mariner's Beach Park?" Ritchie asked. Sheriff Smith took in and let out a deep breath through his nose.

"My advice, I'd steer clear of that story if I were you."

"But this is an important story. I also—

"I think I can see why my friend is annoyed with you. Do what you want, but beware of the hornet's nest you may stir up—you could get stung." And with that, the sheriff walked away.

"Did you hear that, Suzy?"

"Oh, I heard it. And I wish he didn't see us together when he said it. You don't want Smith as an enemy,

Ritchie. Trust me, I know."

"You? What did you ever do?"

"Let's just say in my capacity as an aide I hear things, and what I hear is Sheriff Smith is not someone to tangle with. The fact he apologized to you is astounding. The fact that he warned you off this story... also astounding. That was a gift. If I were you, I'd let it go."

Ritchie glanced at his watch. "Speaking of letting it go, I have to run. I'll see you at softball on Saturday—unless I'm arrested, or worse."

CHAPTER 40

"YOU HAD TO KNOW THIS WAS COMING."

"That's two guys who have died on our watch, dude. It's starting to freak me out."

"Relax. We'll call the doc. He'll come get the liver and then we'll stick the body in the burner, just like we did with the other guy. Only this time we get the liver samples we need to make this whole thing work."

"What if we get caught?"

"Look around, what do you see?"

"A bunch of homeless people with tubes in them waiting to die."

"Okay, when you put it that way it doesn't sound so good. But, like what I meant was, other than the big guy and the doc, nobody knows we're down here. And once we burn the bodies, there'll be no evidence that this ever happened. So chill out, have a beer. I'll call the doctor. Okay? We good?"

"Yeah, I guess. I think I just need a break. It's freakin' cold down here and I haven't seen natural light in a long time. Dude, it's summer. We could be at the beach right now getting waves at The Rock and then hanging with girls. Girls!"

"I know how you feel, bro, but this is easy money."

"I wouldn't call it *easy* money, plus being stuck down here we don't have time to spend what we make. Why don't we trade places with the snatch-and-grab team? Let them watch the stiffs and we can drive the van around and pull people off the streets. How hard can that be?"

"Tell you what. I'll float the idea by the big guy and see what he says. But for now, why don't you get the fire incinerator going so we can make some tasty wood-fired pizzas before we burn the body."

"Dude, you are a sick puppy, you know that?"

His partner didn't answer because he was dialing the doctor who was supposed to come around and check on the "patients" from time to time. But he was such a junkie that he only came when called, and even then he didn't always show up.

CHAPTER 41

ABBY SAT ON HER BED STARING AT THE POSTER on the wall featuring Chargers quarterback Stan Humphries dropping back to pass during their Super Bowl season. Being a "lowly" lineman, Thomas wasn't featured in the photo, but Abby knew it was her father who was effectively blocking one of the Raider rushers in the background. Fortunately, The Don knew too little about football to get the meaning this poster held for Abby. Her walls were covered with football memorabilia, but this poster was her favorite because her dad was doing what he did best—saving someone else from harm. Maybe it was because Thomas was so big that others looked to him for strength, while seeing him broken and beaten like he was since the divorce was hard to handle. She knew her dad took pills for his pain (both physical and mental), and she dealt with the mood swings and other side effects from his injuries (and alcohol), but the single most horrifying experience was when she walked in on her father using a Tazer gun to zap himself to get to sleep. His body shook and his eyes rolled back in his head before he passed out. She never said anything to him, or anyone, about that. Abby preferred to see him the way his fans did, as one of the best blockers in team history, not how he ended up after his playing days were over.

Her trip down memory lane was interrupted by a slight tapping sound on her window. After being followed by a van and knowing what she knew about her stepfather, she was afraid to look—yet the tapping continued. Abby slid off the bed to the floor and crawled up to the window, remaining out of sight. She slowly raised her head and came face to face with her father.

Abby disabled the alarm and opened the window. "Dad, are you crazy? What are you doing here?"

"I want you to come with me."

"Now?"

"Yes, now. But grab a jacket—it's kinda chilly."

"You're worried about me catching a cold? What about getting caught sneaking out of my room? Mom grounded me for life."

"Let's just make sure you don't get sick so Cruella can't add that to the long list of things she thinks I did to you. You can serve out your life sentence after we do what we have to do. This is important and I need your help."

Abby didn't need to be asked twice. She grabbed a hoodie, turned on the television in her room, and climbed out of the ground-floor window, quietly shutting it behind her.

Thomas knew how to sneak around in the shadows to get away unseen. Once they were a block away and safe, he turned to Abby, grabbed her by the shoulders, and asked, "Are you okay?"

"I'm fine. Why?"

"I worry about you. You're twelve going on twenty. When I left you with Ritchie at the beach, I thought it was safer if we were apart. Now I'm not so sure. Either way, I don't want anything to happen to you, so we're sticking together."

"Dad, there is some weird stuff going on, so aren't you right that we're safer apart?. Or is this is just one of your "quality time" things?" The question was a little unfair, since she never minded his wanting to spend time with her. But putting this on him protected her emotionally; she never liked feeling needy.

"Fine, you got me," he admitted after a moment of hesitation. "I want to see more of my little girl."

"I'm not so little anymore," Abby said as she stretched on her toes to show how tall she was, and yet she was still only able to reach up just past her father's chin. But compared to most kids her age, she was tall, and strong, with long legs and an athletic build. She could easily pass for sixteen if she wanted to wear makeup and dress more like a girl, but she liked wearing loose-fitting clothes, which made her look more like a boy—except for her long blonde hair now pulled back in a ponytail.

"Abby, I remember when you were just a baby and I would bounce you in my arms to get you to sleep. I'd just sit in your room after I tucked you in bed. That seems like yesterday. I miss you so much." Abby fell into his arms and he squeezed her tight. "I've missed so much time with you. I hope we can all be together again somehow." Thomas would have stayed like this forever if he could, but they had to keep moving. He handed her a motorcycle helmet. "You're gonna need this."

"Why?" she asked.

"Turn around." Her eyes widened at the sight.

"Are we stealing a motorcycle? Seriously, Dad?"

"No, honey, it's mine."

"Cool!"

"Yeah, cool," Thomas said with a bit of a smile. He hopped on his Harley and Abby sat behind him, wrapping her arms around his waist. He was going to tell her to hang on tight, but she already was. He fired up the bike and put it in gear. "Ready?" He didn't hear Abby's reply because the sound of the awesome machine was so deafeningly loud.

Thomas stuck to the back streets of La Jolla and then Pacific Beach as he headed to Tugs Tavern to meet with Ritchie and share what he'd discovered. He had a few extra minutes to spare, so he decided to go around the block a couple of times to make sure they weren't being followed or walking into a trap. As much as he hated the expression, it was fitting to say the coast was clear, because it literally was—the bar was a short block from the beach. They rode around the back and parked in the alley so they could make a quick escape out the rear door if necessary.

Thomas spotted Ritchie seated in the very back booth of the bar with two attractive women by his side. He figured that's where the reporter would be, but assumed he would be alone.

"Hey, Ritchie, who are these two lovely ladies keeping you company?" Thomas asked.

"Thomas MacDonald, meet Julie Best, my editor."

While the two shook hands, Thomas tried hard not to look too long at Ritchie's boss—but there was something about her that drew him in. She was a petite woman with beautiful brown eyes, straight shoulder-length chestnut hair, and a cute pointed nose. She was dressed casually, but it was her natural beauty that he found attractive. She looked nothing like his ex, which was a good thing.

"It's nice to meet you. I'm a big fan," Julie said as Thomas held her hand a little too long and stared at her. "My dad used to have Chargers season tickets and would take me with him to Jack Murphy Stadium, but that was a long time ago." Julie blushed just a little.

"Yes it was," Thomas acknowledged, getting used to people now telling him their parents saw him play. At least Julie had actually seen him play.

"And on my left," Ritchie continued, "is Lisa, my long-suffering girlfriend."

"I have no doubt," Thomas said with a smile. "It's nice to meet you, and I'm glad Ritchie likes girls his own age." The big man never shied away from blitzing linebackers or the blunt truth.

"And who is the young lady you brought with you, Mr. MacDonald?" Lisa asked as she held out her hand toward Abby.

Thomas was about to say something about not calling him mister and that he was not that old himself, but was spared by Abby speaking first. "I'm Abby, my dad's long-suffering daughter." Everyone laughed. "He has no tact. You're a lot younger than Ritchie." She winked at her father.

"Nice save," Thomas said.

Julie stood up to make room for Abby in the booth. "Abby, I understand you want to be a reporter someday. From what Ritchie says, you're ready right now."

"Thanks. That means a lot coming from you," Abby said.

Lisa nudged Ritchie to move so she could sit next to Abby. "Ritchie told me all about you," she said. "He was right—you really are a smart girl. When I was your age all I cared about was soccer and boys. Do you like—?"

"Yes, she likes soccer," Thomas interrupted while giving Lisa *the look*.

"Riiiighhhhhht," Lisa said, then added, "Why don't you sit down, Mr. MacDonald? You look like you could use a stiff drink."

Ritchie repositioned himself so Thomas could sit down next to him. "Lisa's right. I could use a stiff drink."

"Dad, you're driving me around on a motorcycle. Hello??"

"You are smart," Lisa said. "Let me go get us some drinks from Bullet at the bar. How about sodas all the way around?"

Ritchie groaned, but agreed.

When Lisa left, Ritchie quickly said, "Did you know that Sheriff Smith sent two deputies to my office and told Julie I was wanted for—" he paused, looked at Abby, and said, "for doing things I would never do? Then I ran into the Sheriff at Hobson's bar downtown and he admitted he was doing a favor for a friend. I think we all know who the 'friend' is."

Abby jumped in. "You mean my stepdad."

"Told you she was quick," Ritchie said to Julie.

Julie nodded and added, "The uniformed guys were looking for something on or in Ritchie's desk, but it was such a mess they just gave up and left. I think the whole thing was a ruse to get hold of Ritchie's notes."

"As if I'd leave my notes lying around," Ritchie said as he pointed to his pocket. "I keep them close to the vest."

"Speaking of notes…" Thomas said, before pulling the blueprints out of his backpack and spreading them on the table. "I think we're missing something here." He pointed to a corner of the park on the detailed diagram. "You know what that is?" he asked.

Ritchie, Julie, and Abby shook their heads no.

"This is a huge homeless shelter. This building here is a drug treatment center. Over here, this is affordable housing with enough units for everyone who currently lives in the park. There's more. This building here is designated as a training center—I'm not sure what kind of training, but it could be used for job training. This here is a gym of some kind, this is a laundromat, and over there is a common area with a stage and a park."

Everyone just stared at the plans.

Julie spoke first. "What about these tall building along the water?"

"Those are hotels. Don't get me wrong—there is a lot of commercial and residential development planned for this property, but this whole back area along Rose Creek looks like it's designated for feeding, housing, and possibly teaching the people with nowhere else to go. According to the plans, they will have their own entrance and exit conveniently located right next to a bus line. Then, there's this huge grass area with a hill designed to serve as a natural divide between the two clearly segregated areas—tourists and residents over here, homeless over here." Thomas pointed with his finger on the plan. "This is not what we thought it was—at least not entirely."

Nobody said anything, so Thomas went on. "If I'm reading this right, over here is an area for food trucks, a farmer's market, and a place where people could possible sell their wares in an open-air bazaar. I don't have the details, but it looks like they will use converted shipping containers as temporary spaces for what looks like a coffee shop and other small businesses. There's even a recycling center on site so people won't have to haul their cans and plastics over five miles away to the Midway district for cash. A lot of people will dig that."

"So you're okay with this?" Julie asked.

"Would I rather be living in my van in the same space I've been in for the past couple of years? Yes. Is this the best thing for most of the other residents of the park? I think it is."

"Dad, we both know The Don," Abby said with obvious skepticism on her face. "This doesn't sound like him at all."

"I know. You would think he'd want to squeeze every dollar out of this development deal. That's what he does. But think about it—he's not getting any younger and what's his legacy going to be as it stands now?"

Ritchie was the first to reply. "If I were writing his obituary, it would be about how he built big buildings that obstructed views to the bays and beaches. I probably wouldn't mention this in the piece, but I'm sure a lot of people would be thinking what I am—that he was a ruthless and greedy bastard who would do anything for a buck and as a result was despised by many for many years."

"Exactly!" Thomas said. "Now, if he builds this project the way the plan says he will, he will be remembered as the single biggest backer of the homeless, bar none. His image will change overnight. He'll be a legend in San Diego like Alonzo Horton or George Marston."

"Do you still think he'll make a profit," Ritchie asked, "even with the way this development is designed in these plans?"

"I do. I think it's a win/win for him. First of all, it's the only way this gets approved. Secondly, as I already pointed out, it's a public-relations bonanza. Lastly, look at how many houses he plans to squeeze in here along with the hotels and retail space—and many of these homes will be used by the military. So it's perfect."

"I know the aide I spoke with today said there would be very little political fallout from this," Ritchie said, looking further at the plans, "but she also hinted I should look a little closer into the selection process for who gets chosen to develop their plan for the park. I'm not saying McCallister didn't do anything shady. I'm sure he has, but I did *not* expect this."

"Dad, what about all the people who have disappeared from the park? Do you think The Don had something to do with that?"

"That's what we need to find out," Thomas said.

Julie then chimed in. "Ritchie and I will call around to find out who was on the planning board and selection committee and see what your friend meant when she hinted something was fishy."

Lisa came back with five Cokes, three of which Bullet had spiked with rum. "So what did I miss?"

"A lot. Don't worry, I'll fill you in later," Ritchie said with a wink.

Lisa punched him on the arm and gave him a stern look. "Really, Ritchie? *Really?*"

"What are *we* going to do, Dad?"

"We are going to get a good night's sleep," the big man said to his daughter.

"Where?" Abby asked.

"In my van."

"Is it safe?"

"It is now," Thomas said, thinking back to its perfect hiding place at Web's house.

CHAPTER 42

"WHAT DO YOU MEAN SHE'S NOT IN HER ROOM?" The Don screamed.

"What do you think I mean? She's not there!" Abby's mom yelled back from another room.

"Did the alarm go off at any time tonight?"

"Nope. At least I don't think it did. I took a little nap, okay," she said, even though they both knew she regularly drank herself into a coma.

"You mean you passed out again?" Don said pacing in the hallway outside of Abby's room.

"No, I mean I took a nap."

"Fine, you took a 'nap.' Did you make dinner for Alex before you went to sleep?"

"Of course I... I don't remember, but I'm sure I did."

"Think, Madison, think. When's the last time you saw Abby?"

"When I locked her in her room. I don't know how she could have gone anywhere. Her door was locked from the outside."

Don didn't know what to think. How was it possible she was locked away in her room and now she wasn't there? He walked over to the state-of-the-art security system he'd had installed when he moved in. Primarily to keep his son Ron from entering the house, but also because The Don had made dozens of enemies over the years—including Thomas. He checked the panel, and everything looked normal. He hit the speed-dial button that connected him to the security company that monitored the system and they answered on the second ring.

"Please say your code word," the voice on the other end said.

"Money," was The Don's reply. When the system was set up, they had asked him to say the first word that popped into his head to use for the code.

"And with whom am I speaking?" the security person asked.

"This is Don McCallister."

"Are you okay, Mr. McCallister?" the woman on the other end asked.

"Yes, yes. I gave you the code word. I just want to know something," he said.

"We are not 4-1-1 and the button you pushed is for emergencies only," the dispatcher said, trying to lighten the mood, but The Don didn't get it.

"This *is* an emergency—my daughter is missing!" he screamed.

"Did you call the police?" the dispatcher calmly asked him.

"What? No, she's not missing like that, she's just not home right now."

"How old is your daughter, sir?"

"She's actually not my daughter, but she's twelve… but not the normal kind of twelve, if you know what I mean."

"No, I don't know what you mean. Is she a special-needs child?"

"No!" he answered, irritated that the woman was asking questions instead of providing instant solutions.

"Could she possibly be at a friend's house?"

"No! We locked her in her freakin' room and she was not allowed to leave under any circumstances… for a year," Don yelled to the faceless voice in the box.

"Is it any wonder she left… sir?" the dispatcher asked, unable to resist. "Do you want me to call the police? I think they would be very interested in what's been happening in your house."

"Hang up, Don," Madison, now standing behind him, said very calmly.

"No, I will not hang up! This woman is being disrespectful." Then Don turned his attention from his wife to the intercom and screamed, "Do you know who I am? Do you have any idea who I am? Do you know who I am?"

The woman had heard this before. She'd taken far too many calls from self-important customers who treated her like a servant, and she was perfectly fine risking her job to speak her mind—though in a calm and professional manner.

"So, what you're telling me, sir, is that you tried to imprison a girl who is not your daughter and now you don't have any idea who *you* are. Do you realize how this all sounds? Sir, my advice… hang up immediately and I'll forget you called. Or I can send the police to your residence right now. To tell you the truth, I'm kinda rooting for the girl to get away. The more you tell me, the more worried I am for her safety and the safety of everyone in that house."

The Don lost it and went into one of his infamous tirades where he threatened to ruin the person by having them fired, sue them for all they're worth, and then go after their family for the rest of what he felt they owed him for some slight of some kind—in this case, for humiliating him. Smartly, the dispatcher had already quietly cut the connection before The Don had even finished his first sentence.

"Don, calm down, or you'll give yourself a stroke," Madison said. She then realized the implications of that. *If he had a stroke he could be incapacitated and live for years as a vegetable,* she thought. *No, a fatal heart attack would be much better.*

"Calm down! You want me to calm down? *You* calm down!" he screamed. His surgically altered face turned bright red and the veins on his forehead pulsated with the added blood pressure. "I will not calm down. I bet your husband had something to do with this, didn't he? Are you seeing him on the side? I know you're cheating on me, I know it!"

"Don, you are my husband and Thomas is my *ex*-husband. I haven't seen him since he showed up in court to fight for custody of our kids." Madison sidestepped the general accusation that she was cheating on him. If he ever found out she and his son were romantically involved he would kill them both, which is why she had to kill him first.

"If it's not him, then who is it? Is it that tennis pro at the club? Tell me who it is!" The Don demanded.

"Don't be ridiculous; Jim's gay. We're just friends. My God, what's wrong with you?" Madison asked, trying to push his buttons.

"What's wrong with *me*? With me? What's wrong with *you*? You never want to be together anymore. You stay home all day drinking while I'm out there working my tail off. You aren't going to win any mother-of-the-year awards, that's for sure… or wife of the year, for that matter!"

"Well, you failed as a father your first time around. Your son is so screwed up he's—" Madison stopped herself before she revealed too much. "He's a mess, and it's your fault and it's Diane's fault, too." Madison's calm tone only further infuriated the man.

"You leave my wife out of it! She did the best she could. You don't know anything!"

"Isn't she your *ex*-wife, Don?"

That's when The Don lunged at her throat with both hands.

CHAPTER 43

ENTERING THE PARK BY MOTORCYCLE THE next morning, Thomas and Abby paused to read the announcement stapled to the old guard shack. He idled the engine for a moment of thought, but they needed to keep moving. With his new clean-cut look and helmet on, none of the regulars had a clue it was him, and being seen was not part of his plan. Abby wore a full-face helmet Thomas had borrowed from his teammate's garage to hide her identity. In case someone was waiting for them at his old spot, he rode to the opposite side of the campground to park his Harley. As they walked, they passed the row where his camper van had once been parked and headed to a spot in the back area by Rose Creek. They saw the heavy equipment someone had brought in to intimidate the residents and encourage them to leave—the last step before law enforcement removed them by force. The mechanical beasts loomed large as they sat poised to come to life and level everything in their path.

Walking back through the main grounds, Thomas and Abby passed people who looked like zombies, wandering around and picking through what was left of the abandoned campsites and filling their stolen shopping carts with supplies. After walking up and down two rows, dad and daughter finally found some people they knew.

"Hey, Red, Smokey Joe, Shooter... what's happening?" The three men didn't recognize Thomas right away. "It's me, Big Mac."

"Wow, you clean up pretty good. Oh yeah, and Abby," Red said, suddenly recognizing her and waving hello. His nickname was a no-brainer since his hair was bright red. The other two men's nicknames were also obvious once you knew a little about them. Smokey Joe was a chain-smoker who'd picked up the habit in Vietnam, a place and time that did irreparable damage to his brain—and his lungs. Shooter was much younger, a Special Forces sniper who'd served in Afghanistan and elsewhere in the region during his tours of duty. Red was also ex-military, with the Navy SEALs, but he seldom talked about his service. Finding the three of them together was Big Mac's good fortune because he needed their help and they needed him. They just didn't know it yet.

Thomas explained what he wanted to do and made sure they knew he wouldn't think any less of them if they chose not to help.

CHAPTER 44

"DAD, IT'S ME AGAIN," RON SAID INTO HIS father's voicemail, the sixth message he'd left in a short time. "I'm not sure why you're not picking up, but I have some really good news I want to share with you. Please call me back as soon as you get this."

After hanging up, Ron called Madison. The call went straight to voicemail... again. He debated whether to drive over to the house, but decided that was a bad idea. Instead, he made a couple of calls to his business associates to check on the status of his new venture and to take his mind off being slighted by his father and his stepmother/investor. Things were going along as planned, and he was closer to cashing in on his hard work. Well, hard work in his mind—truth was, he delegated most every aspect of the venture to others. But regardless, he would soon be a success in his own right and earn his old man's respect for what he'd accomplished in just a few months. He would be a successful businessman, just like his father.

CHAPTER 45

SHAGGY WAS BARELY HANGING ON. HE WASN'T sure if he was losing his mind, but it wouldn't be out of the question since he had been strapped down and kept in the dark for what seemed like weeks. When he had a lucid moment, he tried to figure out what the heck was happening to him and the others. He knew they were being used as human guinea pigs, but for what purpose? This led Shaggy to run through in his mind all the terrible diseases they might be injecting him with and it really freaked him out.

He was always skinny, but now without any food and very little water he knew he must be just skin and bones. So instead of fighting against the restraints, he decided he might just be able to wiggle out of them. Sure enough, when he pulled his arm in tight to his body he was able to move it slightly. He then remembered from his Army training that a prisoner could escape from shackles if he broke his own wrists or popped a shoulder out of its socket. The thought made him shudder, but the alternative was more frightening. He may not make it another day. He had to try to free himself and save the others.

Shaggy worked his right arm around to find the

perfect position to pull it free. Every movement caused excruciating pain, but he soldiered on and eventually was able to get his hand out from under the restraint. What he felt for the first time in a long time was hope. He could escape, but he had to hurry. The minute they dosed him up again with drugs, he would be unable to think or act. He kept going and was finally able to bend his arm at the elbow. Now all he had to do was find the release on the strap. He guessed it would be similar to a seatbelt on an airplane. He felt around in the dark for what seemed like a long time but was actually mere minutes.

Then a thought occurred to him. If he could reach the IV and yank it out, he could buy himself more time. He followed the tubes to a spot on his left arm where the needle was taped down and pulled it out. It hurt like heck, but it was a major victory. He celebrated by resting for a few minutes before continuing to work on the strap. Finally, he found the latch and sure enough he was able to loosen it just a little—then a little more.

Eventually, he unshackled his arms and began to work on the leg restraints. All the while, he had to keep perfectly silent, since the place was incredibly quiet and he had no idea if anyone was within earshot. After struggling with the straps, he was finally free—but still confined in the cramped box. He suspected he might be able to put his hands on the top of the tomb and slide the casket-like drawer he was in outward. He wanted to make sure he timed it right, so Shaggy started to slowly and quietly turn himself around in the cramped space. At one point, his chin was in his crotch as he worked himself from feet first to head first where the opening was. Once he was totally turned around, he could see a tiny ray of light coming through the cracks. He was so excited it brought tears to his eyes. He was so close to being free. But he also knew if he wasn't careful, his newfound freedom would be short lived… and so would he.

That's when he had another good idea come to him. He felt around for the IV that was once in his arm and worked his way down the tube until he found the tape and the needle. It was the only weapon he had, but he was so mad at what these people had done to him, it would be all he needed.

CHAPTER 46

RITCHIE AND JULIE QUICKLY REALIZED THEY were no Woodward and Bernstein. Their local sources were better suited for finding out what was happening with beach-area bars rather than what was going on at City Hall. Ritchie tried to reach out to Suzy, but she wasn't taking his calls, probably trying to distance herself and the councilman she worked for from Ritchie and his recent run-in with the law. That's when he had a wild idea. If he found out where the Sheriff lived, he could call him from outside his house and try to rattle his cage and then follow him to see where he went. It sounded like a scene from a tacky television drama, which was why he almost abandoned the idea. Julie came down the steps into her sailboat, cradling her laptop, after being topside while making calls and doing detective work. Ritchie scooted over on the bench seat so she could sit down and put her computer on the tiny table.

"It may be nothing," Julie started saying, while Ritchie got up to get a beer from the small fridge in the galley of the 38-foot Catalina—Julie's home and second office after the divorce. She was able to buy out her husband's share of the newspaper business, but she had to cash in the equity from the beach house the couple had spent seven years renovating; they had turned a small cottage into a three-story showplace worth well over a million dollars. She lost the house and the husband (only one of which she was sorry to see go) but kept her true passions—the newspaper and her sailboat. The boat was supposed to be a temporary space to stay while she regrouped, but she learned to love being a live-aboard in a beautiful marina with other boaters who became her good friends. The lack of a laundry, cold showers, and no true kitchen were a pain, but it was a small price to pay when you can take your home out for a relaxing cruise in the ocean on the weekends.

"Look at this," Julie said, spinning her laptop around so Ritchie could see the picture on the screen.

"Nice house. Is it one of McCallister's properties?"

"It's funny you should ask that, because it *did* belong to him at one time, but he sold it a few years back."

"And… I'm waiting for the other shoe to drop, in the walk-in closet," Ritchie joked.

"Ask me, then," Julie said.

"Okay, who did he sell it to?"

"His good friend—Sheriff Smith. Guess how much it went for?"

Ritchie looked a little closer at the picture of the property and clicked on a couple of other photos before answering. It was a tan, two-story, Spanish-style home with a big brown front door and a small driveway, just a short walk from the beach. The bulk of the house was in back and hidden from view. "I don't know much about real estate except what I read in our own paper, but if I had to guess, I'd say this house is worth around a million. But I'm also guessing that's not what the Sheriff paid for it."

"Good guess. This house is easily worth more than a million, probably more like two million. Look at the location. It's half a block from the beach. From the front it doesn't look like much, which is probably why the Sheriff likes it. Nobody would question it unless they looked at *this* view" Julie said. She then showed Ritchie an overhead satellite shot of the house and the large lot it was located on. "It's a much bigger property than anyone walking by would ever guess."

"Hey, I know this house. It's on Marine Street, and I remember one day during the summer trying to find parking to go to the beach and all of the curbs in front of this house were suspiciously painted red. I was going to do a story about it, but I never got around to it."

Julie rolled her eyes and continued, "Back in 2005, when the housing market was really hot—which I remember because we sold almost all of our ad space to Realtors back then—this house sold for $500,000."

"Man, I could've almost afforded that," Ritchie said.

Julie just looked at him.

"What?" he said.

"I know what I pay you, most of which you spend on beer, and I doubt you could have swung it, except that this particular house was purchased with no money down. Zip."

"Did McCallister give the house to his buddy as a gift?"

"Yes and no. Because the sheriff is an elected official, he cannot accept a $500,000 gift. So somehow The Don figured out a way to make it look like the house went through escrow and monthly payments are being made by the sheriff, but I doubt he even pays the property taxes on it."

"Interesting. I kind of remember him telling me at Hobson's that he owed a favor to a friend. Now I think I know what it was for."

"You're talking about the sheriff, right?"

"Yeah, yeah. Smith said that when he bought me a beer."

"I'm not sure how all of this ties into your story, but it will certainly make for interesting reading when this whole homeless park business is put to rest. So, your car or mine?"

"Julie, no offense, but you can't just hop into your Mercedes without opening the door. With my Mustang, you can. So let's ride."

"When you speak to me like that like that I have to wonder why I ever hired you as a reporter. Fine, we'll take your car—even though it is highly conspicuous."

"Hey, Magnum P. I. did stakeouts in a bright-red Ferrari 308, so we can manage in my bright-red Mustang 302. How will we know if the sheriff is home?"

"I happen to know what kind of car he drives," Julie said.

"Really, how did you find that out?"

"Think, Ritchie, think."

"You looked it up?"

"No—he drives a police cruiser. Duh. We just need to see if it's in the driveway."

"Why wouldn't he park it in the garage?"

"Do you ever pay attention to detail?" Julie asked.

"What detail did I miss?"

"Remember the overhead shot of his house I showed you?"

"Yeah."

"Did you happen to notice a green-and-white cruiser backed into the driveway?"

"If I say yes will you believe me?"

"No. But at least we're on the same page now. Since the house has a garage, I'm guessing he keeps it out there to deter any burglars who have no idea whose house it is." Ritchie nodded in agreement.

"Julie, you really are the best boss."

"You're just saying that again because it's my last name."

"This time I think I mean it."

CHAPTER 47

THE WHITE PANEL VAN CRUISED ALL THE USUAL places looking for at least one or two new homeless targets to pick up and take back for testing, since two had just died and they needed more liver samples to submit. There were fewer people out and about, so the team turned around and decided to drive right to the park to pursue their quarry. Part of the thrill for the sadistic kidnap crew was the hunt. Once they homed in on a homeless man wandering around alone, the snatch-and-grab part was easy. Shaggy had put up quite a fight, but most everyone else they'd kidnapped almost came willingly—though using a sedative helped ensure their silence. So far they had only tried to snag one person at a time, so grabbing two would be an interesting new challenge.

It took a while, but they finally found an older red-headed man stumbling along a path near the park. It was the perfect place to pick him up since the road was rarely driven on and it was lined with overgrown bushes that blocked the view of prying eyes and those who might be on the other side. The remoteness also made it unlikely anyone would be within earshot in case something went awry and they couldn't quickly quiet their prey.

They were bummed they couldn't get two at a time, but one would do for now— and they could always come back for a second person after dropping this one off. The occupants of the van prepared themselves for the takedown, driving ahead of the old man and then waiting by the side of the road nearest the path. They watched in the rear-view mirror as he stumbled toward them, completely unaware of the fate awaiting him. As he neared the rear of the van, he stopped and the team swung the side door open. To their astonishment, he was gone.

In a flash, Red had gotten under the van and crawled his way to the driver's side. He'd done many missions similar to this one in Vietnam, but back then, he was crawling through the jungle to ambush the enemy—today he was crawling in the dirt to ambush the enemy. Red got ready and watched the feet of the two men who had jumped out of the van. Then, just as planned, two other pairs of feet ran into view, there was a momentary struggle, and the two kidnappers went down. That's when he saw Shooter and Smokey Joe quickly and expertly silence the two men using the military training they'd never forgotten. He wasn't sure what method they used, and he wasn't sure he wanted to know, but it worked. Now it was time for him to put his part of the plan in action.

As expected, the driver of the van got out to see what had happened. As soon as his feet hit the ground, Red yanked them out from under him, and within a second he scampered on top of the guy. In one movement, Red sat upright and delivered a hammer of a punch to the man's temple. The man went limp and his eyes closed. Not bad, Red thought to himself.

Red stood and dragged the driver to the back of the van, where Shooter and Smokey Joe were securing the other two men using the kidnappers' tools of the trade from the van—duct tape and zip ties.

"Here's the driver," Red said, propping the guy's limp body against the bumper. "I think he's out cold, but I haven't hit anyone like that in a long time. He could just be dazed."

Shooter quickly zip-tied the driver's hands behind his back and then pulled off his mask. "Red, look at this—he's just a kid."

"I guess I still got it," Red said proudly. He'd taken down someone half his age and twice his size.

"Red, what I mean is, this guy is barely in his twenties," Shooter said.

Smokey Joe had a crazed look in his eyes. Clearly, he was loving being back in action and thankfully he wasn't armed. He ripped the masks off the other two men but had no reaction. Shooter and Red did, though.

"What the heck?" Red said. "Is this some kind of a prank? Grab some homeless guys and then rough them up? I don't get it. What did these kids do with all the people who disappeared from the park?"

"What if we've got the wrong guys?" Smokey Joe said.

"Nah. I bet this is who we're looking for," Shooter said. "I say we take 'em somewhere so we can spend some quality time together and find out what's really going on." He turned to Red. "You wanna drive or should I?"

"You drive, I'll stay in the back and make sure Smokey Joe doesn't kill 'em before we get a chance to torture them to death."

Upon hearing his name, Smokey Joe instinctively reached in the pocket of his Army jacket and pulled out a cigarette butt and lit it. With the price of smokes so high, Smokey Joe spent his days looking for and collecting discarded cigarettes, saving any new ones he got for special occasions.

"Sounds good to me," he said between puffs. "I learned a couple of very effective interrogation techniques during my time in 'Nam. Unfortunately, some of them were used on me." Smokey Joe let out a crazy, throaty laugh.

CHAPTER 48

"DAD, WHAT DID YOU DO WITH MY PHONE?" Abby asked while she searched the van and the garage it was now parked in.

"I hid it someplace safe, and I'll give it back to you when this is all over. We can't take any chances on people following us around using GPS or something. What do you need your phone for anyway?"

"I was thinking it would be a good idea to call Mom and tell her where I am." Her father raised his eyebrows when she said "where." Abby quickly corrected herself. "I mean tell her *how* I am, that I'm okay, not *where* I am. What if she freaks out and calls the cops?"

"I think she has a good idea you're with me. I'm still your father, and I should be able to spend some quality time with my daughter."

"But—"

"I hear you, honey, but we can't risk it. We don't know who we can trust right now."

"Maybe we should just go to the police with what we know."

"Or… the F-B-I," Thomas said, almost to himself.

"The FBI?" Abby asked.

"The FBI. Yeah. I almost forgot. Three agents tried to

jump me at the beach the other day."

"What?? And you can actually forget such a thing?"

"With everything going on—" Abby cut him off.

"Dad, you really make me wonder sometimes." The words cut deeper than she had any clue; she sounded just like her mom. "Okay, so why would FBI agents jump you at the beach?"

"I don't know. I didn't give them a chance to talk." Abby had her own *look* that she sometimes gave her dad, as she did now. "I did what I had to. Look, what do I know that would make the Feds want to talk to me? Nothing, right? But I must know something or else they wouldn't have been waiting for me when I got out of the water."

"Maybe they wanted your help," Abby pointed out.

"Hmmm. I never thought of that. I doubt they do now. But what would they need me for? They have the power of the federal government behind them. Wait a minute. Wait… a… minute." Abby could see the wheels turning in her dad's mind. "Let's think about all the people we know who've gone missing. What do they all have in common?"

"They were all homeless," Abby quickly answered.

"Okay, right, but beyond that?" Abby thought for a moment and then shrugged. "Honey, they were almost all ex-military. Maybe they were kidnapped so someone could collect on their government checks. I know Shaggy got money every month from the Navy. It wasn't much, though. But if we added all the checks together…" He paused as he thought twice about his theory. "Hmm… I guess it wouldn't be worth the trouble to kidnap—or kill—that many people. Okay, I don't know, it doesn't really hold up."

"So, are you saying you *don't* think the missing people were forced out by The Don?"

"Well, we can't rule that out, but where would he keep them? He'd need to have help. I mean, it could be that the whole homeless village part of the plans is just for show and will be swapped out after they're approved, but I don't think so. I think The Don is using this project to improve his image and make a profit. If it came out he somehow did something to the very people he planned to help, it would ruin his reputation forever. No, it would be too risky."

"So what do we do now?"

"I have an idea. You're going to write a letter to the FBI." Thomas paced alongside his van in the garage.

"But I don't have a computer," Abby pointed out.

"You don't need one. You're going to write it with paper and pen and we'll send it through the post office."

"Dad, you're such a dinosaur."

"We have to use what we have, and believe it or not, this will make it harder for them to trace it back to us."

"But why are we even writing to the FBI?"

"We need their help. Let's put them and all their resources on The Don's case and sit back and see if they figure out what he's done or not done in the development deal."

"You think they'll really look into his dealings just based on a handwritten letter from some girl?"

"They will if you write what I tell you to write."

CHAPTER 49

"RON, GET HOLD OF YOURSELF! FOR GOD'S SAKE, calm down."

Ron knelt over his father's dead body, rocking back and forth, sobbing uncontrollably and mumbling over and over, "Dad, I did it all for you. I did it all for you."

"Ron, we need to—"

That's when Ron snapped, leapt up, and grabbed Madison by the shoulders, shaking her like rag doll as he screamed, "You killed him! You killed him!"

"Ron... wait... no. He was... choking me and—" This was all Madison could get out before Ron's rage overcame him and he lost control.

"You killed my father! Why? Why?" Ron screamed as spit flew out of his mouth like a rabid dog as he raged just inches from her face.

"He was trying to kill me, I swear. I—" Ron's fist hit her head so hard that her world instantly went black. Her slack body fell backward and her head smacked against a small table, opening up a gash in her forehead that began bleeding profusely.

Alex heard the commotion in the hall, but was terrified to leave his room. First he heard his mother and stepfather fighting and then he heard his mother and stepbrother arguing. His mother and stepfather often fought and he heard them say awful things to each other, but he always figured it was better to pretend like he never heard a thing. That's what he would do tonight—put his headphones on and act like he never heard a word. Then someone began pounding on his door.

"Alex! I need you to come out here and see what your mom did to my dad. Now!" Ron yelled like a crazed person.

Alex decided to pretend he couldn't hear, but seconds later, his door exploded into pieces as Ron kicked it in and off its hinges. Alex sat frozen on his bed, recoiled into a ball against the headboard. Ron grabbed him by his arm and yanked him out into the hallway where the two bodies were crumpled on the floor.

"Mom! Mom!" Alex tried to run to his mother, but Ron held him back.

"Your mom," Ron said with a sneer, "killed my dad. Did you know that? Did you?"

"Let me go. What did you do to my mom?"

"Nothing she didn't deserve. Now, where's your pretty little sister?"

"She's not here."

"Well, I think it's time we go and find her and make her pay for what her mother did to my dad. An eye for an eye."

"Leave my sister alone! She didn't do anything to *you*!"

"Fine, then I'll get my revenge on you."

"No. Nooooooo!" Alex wailed as he burst into tears.

"Then you and I are going to go hunt down Abby

and bring her back here."

"What about my mom?" Alex cried out, looking at the pool of blood spreading around her head and feeling his knees buckle. "Is she going to be okay?"

"Not if I can help it," Ron said.

CHAPTER 50

AFTER JUST A FEW MINUTES, THE KIDNAPPERS realized three things. One, these three homeless guys were crazy. Two, they were very strong and able to inflict a kind of pain they'd never felt before. Three, they would be dead if they didn't cooperate… so they did.

"Please, no more," one of the kidnappers muttered as Smokey Joe prepared to deliver another blow to the young man's groin. "I'll tell you whatever you want to know." Then he puked from the previous punch to his privates.

"That's too bad. I was looking forward to torturing you a little bit more. I miss it, you know. The smell of burning skin from a lit cigarette pushed deep into a cheek. Ah, the good old days." Smokey Joe meant every word, and the terror in the boys' eyes was real as they watched the vet take a long drag from his smoke.

As the first kidnapper remained slumped over, with thick vomit still dropping from his lips, one of the others decided to speed this up. "Your friends are all being held at the old hospital in La Jolla," he quickly said. "We'll take you there, I swear. Please don't burn me, Mr. Joe. Smokey. Mr. Smokey. Please."

"Whaddya think, Shooter? Should we let him live?"

Shooter didn't say a word, instead giving a simple thumbs-down. The kidnapper saw it and panicked. "Please, no! I don't want to die. Plus, you need me to get into the building."

"We can have your friend get us in when he wakes up," Shooter said. "If he wakes up." Shooter looked down at the sprawled body of the driver, still out cold. "Wow, Red, you really pack a punch. This one's still unconscious, or maybe he's dead." Nobody had bothered to check his pulse.

CHAPTER 51

"SMITTY, YOU KNOW ME. I WOULDN'T HURT anyone. You gotta believe me," Ron said to the sheriff, who was also his godfather. The two men were standing inside the living room of Smith's mini mansion while Alex was seated on the couch with headphones on so he couldn't hear the conversation.

"Ron, I want to believe you, but I've been at this longer than you've been alive and your story doesn't make sense. Why in the world would your dad want to hurt your stepmother?"

"Because Madison and I were having an affair and he found out," Ron admitted.

"What!? No, that can't be. No. No. No," the sheriff said emphatically.

"It's true. When I told my dad, he lost all control and went after my stepmom and started strangling and beating her and then he just stopped."

"Because he had a heart attack, you said?"

"Or a stroke, I don't know. He just started gasping for air and then collapsed on top of her."

"What did you do?"

"I got Alex out of there and came straight here."

"See, an innocent person would've called 911. An

innocent person would have waited for the police to arrive. An innocent person would have tried to revive his father and check to see if his stepmother was still breathing and, if she wasn't, administered CPR. Or at least tried to. You didn't do any of those things, did you, Ron?"

"I guess I panicked."

"And why didn't your dad try to strangle you? I mean, you also betrayed him, and let's be honest, he wasn't your biggest fan."

"Because he was afraid of me?" Ron offered.

"That's the first thing you've said I believe. Here's what's going to happen. Ron, you and I are going to go back to the house, and I will make a determination about what to do with you based on what I see. Alex will stay here."

"Alone?"

"No, I'll have my neighbor's kid come over and watch him."

"Fine. But I want to drive myself."

"Out of the question. You're not calling the shots here. You're coming with me until we can sort this all out."

"Are you calling in backup?"

"Not now. I will be the first on the scene and make a determination of what to do then."

"Okay, then I'll ride with you."

"It isn't a choice, Ron." The sheriff then went to the phone on the table by the sofa.

"Whatever you say," Ron replied. A moment later, the sheriff turned his back to call his neighbor, and Ron took the chance to grab a heavy community-service award displayed on the sideboard. He lifted it high and then brought it down hard on the back of the sheriff's head. The big man went down in a heap. "Sorry, but it has to be this way, Smitty." Ron grabbed the horrified Alex and bolted for the door.

There was no turning back now. He'd just assaulted an officer of the law—as if kidnapping and murder weren't bad enough.

CHAPTER 52

"THIS IS THE PLACE," JULIE SAID AS SHE PARKED on the street. "Wow, it really is deceiving, looking from here. You truly can't tell how big the place is."

"You know what they say?"

"What do they say, Ritchie?"

"Location, location, location."

"They also say size doesn't matter," Julie added, "but I'd argue that it does."

"Are we still talking about real estate?"

"Yes. Now let's go knock on the door and have a chat with the sheriff."

But before they could even get out of the car, the front door of the sheriff's house burst open and a tall man towing a young boy by the arm ran out, got into a brown van, and sped away.

"Julie, follow them! I'll go inside and see what happened." Ritchie jumped out of the Mustang convertible over the door, while Julie hopped in the driver's seat and took off in pursuit of the van.

Ritchie had no idea what he might be walking into. Logically, his brain told him not to go inside—his motto to young journalists was always, "Report the news; don't *be* the news." As he crouched behind a bush, trying to see into the slightly open front door, he reached for his phone to call 911. But it hit him that this was the home of one of the highest-ranking law enforcement officers in San Diego. Screw it—he was going in. Tonight, his right brain would rule and he would throw caution to the wind.

Ritchie found Sheriff Smith lying on the floor in the living room. He couldn't tell if he was dead or alive, so he did what they do on television—he felt for a pulse on his neck. It wasn't as easy as they made it look on TV. Maybe he felt something. He wasn't sure. So he put his ear to the sheriff's nose to listen for breathing. Ritchie let out a sigh of relief as he confirmed the man to be alive. *Thank God,* he thought. The last thing he needed was to be found crouching over the dead body of the sheriff.

Ritchie began looking over the inert body for signs of trauma. Was he shot? Stabbed? Strangled? All he could say for sure was that he was out cold. He was reluctant to roll him over, not just because he was a heavy man, but also because they always say to never move an injured person unless you have to. He managed to roll him enough on his side to see his holster and gun in the small of his back. *That's curious,* he thought. *Why didn't he use it on the person who attacked him? Maybe he knew the man.* The lawman's smartphone was by his side, but it was password protected, so Ritchie couldn't find anything there. At that moment, he decided he'd better call 911 when, of all things, the doorbell rang.

"Nobody's home," he called out in a moment of panic.

A young girl's voice called back, "If nobody's home,

who are you?"

Ritchie rolled his eyes at his own stupidity, then walked to the door. Through the peephole he saw Thomas and Abby.

"I didn't do it," was the first thing Ritchie said to them as he opened the door.

"What didn't you do?" Thomas asked as his large frame came through the doorway.

"That," Ritchie said pointing to the body lying on the floor.

"Oh, that," Thomas replied, looking at the inconvenient scene before him.

"Is he, like, dead?" Abby asked, not sure she wanted to know the answer.

"He's breathing, but I don't know what happened to him. I found him this way. A tall guy and a boy ran out just as Julie and I got here."

Thomas and Abby looked at each other. "What did the kid look like?"

Ritchie described what sounded exactly like Alex.

"Was he okay?" Thomas urgently asked.

"I think so. I know the kid didn't look happy, that's for sure."

"That's my son, Alex—Abby's brother." Thomas's jaw clenched with a tinge of anger.

"Dad, I bet it's Ron who has him. Ritchie, what did the tall guy look like?"

Ritchie described Ron perfectly, and as bad as the situation was, Thomas and Abby were a bit relieved it wasn't a stranger.

"Why are you two here?" Ritchie asked, suddenly

realizing the randomness of their showing up at Sheriff Smith's house.

"We wanted to talk to the sheriff. We knew he had to be connected in some way to what was going on, but we couldn't be sure until we met with him face to face."

"Maybe you can still have that talk. I haven't called the police, and I think he's just unconscious. Seems he was knocked out with that big plaque on the floor."

"Let me take a look at him," Thomas said. "I know a little something about head trauma from my playing days." The big man examined the smaller big man and then went into the kitchen, returning a couple minutes later with supplies—specifically, a pitcher of ice water. Once Thomas poured it on the face of the sheriff, he immediately came back to consciousness.

"What the—?" He quickly propped himself up on one elbow, as his eyes blinked and looked around, trying to focus on something, anything. A few moments later, he recognized Ritchie and looked at him, confused.

"You were out cold," Ritchie said. "What happened?"

The three of them helped the sheriff up and onto the couch. He rubbed the back of his head and cursed to himself before he spoke.

"I can't believe I let that punk get the jump on me. I must be slipping. Thomas, I'm sorry to say, but he has your son."

"That's what Ritchie said. I'm gonna freakin' kill that kid."

Sheriff Smith gave him a look that let him know he was still the law.

"I'll kill him slowly," Thomas said with a raised eyebrow.

"There will be no killing." Then the sheriff paused for a moment in a realization. "Oh my God… I just remembered why Ron came here in the first place. Abby, could you go into the kitchen and grab me a cold beer from the fridge? It's that way, through those doors."

"Okay." She looked at her dad with a puzzled expression on her face, to which he just shrugged.

Once she was gone, the sheriff said in a slightly hushed tone, "Ron came here with a crazy story about Don having a stroke or heart attack while he was strangling Madison to death."

"You don't believe him?" Ritchie asked.

"I've known Ron all his life and he's a pathological liar. I was on my way to check it out when he hit me from behind."

"Where was Alex when all of this happened?" Thomas asked.

"I don't know, but he was with Ron when he came here. All I know is we'll get some answers at Don's house, one way or another."

Abby came back with a beer and handed it to the Sheriff. He drank it in one long swig and said, "I don't think I should be driving. Do any of you have a car?"

"Julie went after Ron and Alex in my Mustang, and I stayed behind," Ritchie said.

"We're on a Harley, sheriff," Thomas said, pointing to Abby.

"Call me Smitty. Okay, one of you gets to drive the cruiser."

Ritchie didn't hesitate: "I've always wanted to drive a police car."

"Okay. No lights or sirens, and I am absolutely not sitting in the back," Sheriff Smith said.

"Fair enough. It looks like you're my prisoner, Abby," Ritchie said, trying to be funny.

Ritchie's phone rang and everyone jumped. Ritchie looked down and saw it was Julie, so he put her on speaker phone. "Julie, where are you?"

"I'm following the van. They drove around like they thought they were being followed, then they parked not that far from you."

"You mean they're outside the sheriff's house?"

"Not exactly. They're parked on the street in front of the Bishop's School."

The sheriff spoke up, "Yeah, that's pretty close to here."

"Julie, I'm on my way to you," Thomas said. "If they move, follow them and text your location to this number." Thomas read off the number to his burner phone.

"Okay, what's happening over there?" she replied.

"It's a long story," Ritchie answered. "We're heading over to Abby's house right now. I'll fill you in when we get there."

"You said it's a long story. Is it going to be one with a happy ending?"

"It depends whose perspective you're looking at it from. I can't really talk right now; we've gotta go. Thomas is on his way to you."

"I'll keep an eye out for him and keep an eye on your brother, Abby."

"Thank you, Julie," the girl said.

Ritchie hung up and Thomas said, "Abby, like we said, go with the sheriff and Ritchie, and I'll go get Alex."

"MacDonald," the sheriff said, "be smart. You don't want to kill anyone, no matter what he may have done."

"Who said anything about killing?"

"You did."

Thomas ignored the reply and ran for the door to save his son.

CHAPTER 53

"WHAT'S UP, DOC?" ONE OF THE TWO BOZOS guarding the patients asked the disgraced doctor as he walked in.

"Doesn't that ever get old?" the doc asked back.

"Nah, not really." "So what have we got here?" the doc asked.

"Beer?"

"No, I'm referring to the… Geez. I need the charts!"

"Yeah, about that…" the other bozo started. "We're getting bored. Isn't there some way to speed this up so we can get paid?"

"Don't I wish. Charts?"

"That's the thing. We kinda stopped monitoring the stiffs, hoping they would just die, so you could harvest their livers and we can cash in and get outta here."

"How did I ever get mixed up with you idiots?"

"I think we both know how. What we should focus on is how to get to the finish line faster."

"We can't rush this or it won't work," the doctor said flatly. "So let's do this the right way so this wasn't a big waste of time."

"Fine… start with the scrawny guy. I doubt he's even still alive."

"What drawer?" the doc asked. One of the guys pointed to the drawer containing Shaggy.

"Hey," the other guy said, "do you mind if we go out for smoke while you do what you gotta do?"

"Fine, go."

The two guys happily went outside while the doctor grabbed the clipboard containing Shaggy's chart. He looked it over for a minute, then walked over to refrigerator drawer number 12. Still scrutinizing the stats on the chart, he pulled the drawer handle. He never saw the needle coming as Shaggy expertly shoved the sharp part of the intravenous tube into the fleshy part of the doctor's face before he could react. While the doctor was screaming and grabbing for the needle, Shaggy rolled out and tried to run but his legs were like wet noodles and wouldn't work—so he crawled across the floor.

"You can't leave. I need your liver!" the doctor yelled.

Shaggy was starting to get the feeling back in his legs in sharp pains like needles. He pulled himself up and was walking while holding onto the wall trying to get away from the doctor. Though weak and struggling, he was getting closer to the door when the doctor came running up the ramp, his hand covering the puncture wound on his face.

"You can't leave," the doc called from behind.

"Watch me," Shaggy said as he burst through the double doors and out onto the sidewalk, not sure where he was or what day it was. All he knew was that it was nighttime and the darkness would help him escape.

Had anyone been on the deserted street, it would

have been quite a sight to see the emaciated, naked man stumbling along the sidewalk. The two guys on smoke break didn't, because they were around back. And the doctor knew better than to follow him—more urgent to destroy any and all evidence of his involvement in the human testing.

Shaggy, meanwhile, had no idea where he was heading; he just wanted to get as far away from the building as he could. He was so disoriented that, when he heard a somewhat familiar voice call out his name, he thought he was hallucinating. It'd been so long since he'd seen light that the one streetlamp overhead burned into his eyes like the sun. Then, he heard the voice again.

"Shaggy! Hey, Shaggy!" Red yelled from the kidnappers' van, just as he was turning the corner near their destination. But the naked, skinny guy just kept walking away.

During the drive, Shooter had punched one of the two young punks in the throat—a good move if you want to incapacitate someone, but not so good if you need the person to talk. "Is this the place?" Shooter asked.

The kid gurgled a "yes," so the crew slowed down as they went past the old building to get to their friend.

"That sure seems like Shaggy," Red said. "You guys, open the slider and grab the guy."

Shaggy, however, wasn't about to get taken by the same van again—and after he'd just escaped, no less. So he jumped over a row of bushes to disappear. The damp grass felt good on his bare skin, as he curled up in a ball and tried to hide. But Red could see through the bushes that the guy was right there, just behind the branches and leaves.

Red stopped the van and hunched over the steering wheel to contemplate what he thought he'd just seen. *Was that really Shaggy? Why didn't he respond to his name or reach out for help? And why is he naked?* Red turned back to his captives and said, "What did you do to our friend?"

"We were testing a new drug and needed liver samples to get funding," said the guy who could still talk most clearly.

"What kind of testing? What kind of drug?" Red demanded.

"I don't know. All I know is nobody was supposed to get hurt."

"Really? Well, you know what?" Red asked.

"What?" the guy asked with hesitation.

"I'm thinking of doing a clinical trial of a new drug I like to call 'Severe Pain,'" Red said with a straight face.

"That doesn't sound like something Big Pharma would take to market," Smokey Joe joked.

"Yeah, probably not, but I'm just curious to see how tough today's youth is," Red said and smiled.

And with that, the three homeless people began beating on the two kidnappers and didn't stop until they were unconscious like their partner.

After observing Shaggy for a bit, Red concluded his skinny friend was probably drugged and delirious, and possibly paranoid. Smokey Joe and Shooter agreed and decided they'd best take him by surprise. But when the two came up from behind him with a blanket, he was too exhausted to even try to get away. They simply wrapped up the slight man and carried him back to the white van. They carefully placed him in the cargo area, doing their best to make him comfortable.

"When I saw this van I thought you were those guys, gonna get me again," Shaggy said, looking up with the fearful eyes of a lost puppy.

"Nope. We're here to save you," Smokey Joe said.

"I'm not the only one they have in there." Shaggy groaned as they set him down.

"We know. Tell us where they are and we'll go get 'em out," Shooter said.

Shaggy looked out and pointed to the doors he had run through a few minutes earlier. Shooter and Smokey Joe took off toward the closed medical facility. Shaggy then curled up in a corner of the van and closed his eyes, seemingly oblivious to the three unconscious and bound kidnappers on the other side of the cargo space.

"What happened in there?" Red asked.

Shaggy just shook his head.

"You look like you could use something to drink. I know I could." Red rummaged through the three kids' pockets and pulled out their wallets, which were flush with cash. "Hey! It looks like we're gonna be livin' large for the next couple of days."

"Think again, loser!" Red heard someone say. He then turned his head to see Ron pointing a handgun at him through the driver's side window. "You aren't going to be living large because you aren't going to be living at all if you don't give me those wallets and let my friends go."

Red had no options, being far enough from the gun that he couldn't get any move off quicker than he'd be shot. He reluctantly handed over the wallets. "Your buddies are a little worse for wear, I'm afraid. I think they both fell down and hit their heads."

"Show me," Ron said with the gun still pointed directly at Red's head.

Red reached over and opened the sliding door. One of the two young guys rolled out onto the street while the other just hung there, half in and half out of the van.

Ron aimed his pistol at each one and fired two rounds into their heads. "No loose ends." He then saw Shaggy, who was trying to play dead but was visibly trembling. "Who is that?"

"Him, oh, he is a friend of mine. He's barely alive, so leave him alone."

Ron aimed his gun but never got a shot off. From behind, Thomas blazed by on his motorcycle with one leg out, foot up, and planted it right on Ron's back side, smashing him into the side of the van and then onto the ground.

Thomas skidded his Harley to a stop and let it fall to the pavement. His left leg ached from the impact with Ron's behind, making him look even more menacing as he limped up the street toward Ron's limp body.

Red stepped out of the van to meet Big Mac. "Thanks, bro. You saved my life."

"What the heck is going on here?" Thomas asked.

Red pointed to the interior of the van where Shaggy was shivering under a blanket.

"Shaggy?" Thomas wondered.

"We need to get him to a hospital. A real hospital," Red said.

"Shaggy, hang in there, buddy. Help is on the way," Thomas said into the van before he turned and walked toward Ron, whom he had only met once or twice before.

Thomas rolled Ron over onto his back with his foot, then searched for the gun. It wasn't in Ron's hand, so Thomas looked around for it. It was just a few feet away in the wet grass. Thomas picked the gun up, released the clip, and put the clip in his pocket., He then ejected the bullet in the chamber and tossed it down a nearby drain. He walked over to Ron, who was now sitting up, and stood tall over the little man while pointing the gun at him.

"You gonna shoot me?" Ron said. "You can't do that. You'll go to prison forever."

"Seeing you dead would be worth it."

"But what about Abby and Alex? Please just don't shoot me. Call the cops. I'll give up."

"Let's have a little agreement—you explain all this, and I won't shoot you." Thomas stared into Ron's eyes with the same look he gave defensive linemen in the NFL. But they knew it was just a game, while Ron was playing for his life.

"Okay," Ron said with a nod.

"First, where's Alex?" Thomas asked back.

"He's fine. He's in that van over there." Ron gestured to the lone vehicle parked across the street.

"What did Alex ever do to you, Ron?"

"What did he do? What did he do?"

"That's what I asked. Or would you prefer to try to

answer with a bullet hole in your face?"

"No, no! It's just that he… well, he… he, he, he was my father's favorite."

"So you resented him, is that it?" Thomas said.

"I was never good enough for my father. I know that. He thought I was a no-good, lazy waste of space."

"So you planned to kill your dad?"

"No! I did all of this for *him*."

"All what, Ron? What did you do?"

"I helped him with his problem."

"And what problem is that?" Thomas inched the gun nearer to Ron's head to emphasize his need for an answer.

"You know, the homeless problem at the point. I made them disappear."

"How did you do that?"

"My friends and I took them here," Ron said pointing at the building behind them. "Then we did testing on them for a new drug being developed that can regenerate a liver, even one that's been badly abused for years. It'll be worth millions. Hundreds of millions, and I'm in on the ground floor." Just then, Ron's face shifted with a realization, and he sat up a little straighter. "Mr. MacDonald, I can get you in on this, too—you could be rich again!"

The words barely left Ron's lips before Thomas kicked him in the chin at the mere thought of this idea. Ron shook his head slightly to regain his senses, then dabbed his fingers to the blood dribbling down his chin. He looked back up at Big Mac.

"I should shoot you just for saying that," Thomas

told him.

"No! We had a deal!"

"Right! So tell me—are all the people you took for testing your new wonder drug still in there?"

"No, some of them didn't make it and we had to—" Ron thought better of mentioning they were incinerated. "We had to take them to a funeral home."

"One last question, and then we're done. Did your dad know about all this?"

"No, not at all. I swear. It was going to be a surprise. But your… uh… Madison, she did. She was my biggest backer." As badly as Thomas thought of her, even he didn't see that coming. It wasn't even possible for him to process that information right now. The woman he'd married, the mother of his kids. As his mind started to spin at the thought, Ron continued. "She didn't feel like my dad paid enough attention to her. He barely gave her any money to spend. This plan was how we could both make things right. He'd respect me, and we'd have the money he would never share. So, I'm not a bad person. This was—"

"Shut up and stand up," Thomas interjected.

"Are you going to call the cops now?"

"I said stand up!" Ron nodded quickly and scampered to his feet.

"Enough talking, it's time for you to die." Thomas pressed the muzzle of the gun between Ron's eyes.

"You… you… you…" Ron stammered to get the words out as he gasped to catch his breath. "You said we had a deal. I told you everything."

"Yes, you did," Thomas said, "But you still need to

die." And with that, he pulled the trigger. Amidst the roar of adrenaline in his body, Ron heard the click and then silence. His eyes were smashed shut, waiting for the blow that never came. Now, all he heard was the pounding of the blood vessels in his head. Slowly, he opened his eyes and let out his breath. Thomas lowered the gun and Ron started to breathe in spasms of relief.

"You... you... you're honoring our deal?" he said.

"Correct. I'm not going to shoot you."

"Oh my God. Thank you. Thank you."

"But you've still got a ticket to hell." A puzzled look crossed Ron's face just before Thomas stepped closer and executed his signature move—a quick blow to the throat. The kid reached for his crushed windpipe, then Thomas unleashed a trio of fast and powerful blows that sent Ron to the ground in a lifeless lump. Thomas stood over him for a moment, before Red walked over and kicked the kid in the head. Ron never felt it, though, because he was dead on his feet after the second and third strikes from Thomas landed on his temple and solar plexus.

"Big Mac, "Red said, "didn't your mom ever tell you it's wrong to throw trash in the street?"

"Well, this trash we have to leave here." Thomas pulled the ammo clip from his pocket, put it back in the gun, and loaded a round into the chamber. Then, after wiping his fingerprints from it with his shirt, he put the gun into Ron's rubbery right hand. "I'll grab Shaggy and bring him over to that other van. I have to make sure my son is okay. You wipe down anything you touched and get my bike, okay?"

"What about the others?" Red asked.

"First things first.—my son, Shaggy, and getting rid of any evidence we were here. Were Shooter and Smokey Joe with you?"

"Oh yeah. They went inside."

"All right. When you're done, go get those two, and we'll call the authorities—but we were never here, okay?"

"Got it."

Thomas picked Shaggy up and carried him toward the Ron's van, worried what he would find when he opened the door.

CHAPTER 54

"SHERIFF, CAN I SPEAK WITH YOU ALONE?" THE emergency room doctor asked. Sheriff Smith, Abby, and Ritchie had gone to Abby's house, where Smith quickly assessed the situation before calling in a medic unit for Abby's mom and the San Diego police to work the crime scene.

"I want to stay," Abby said. "I can handle it, whatever it is. I can handle it."

The doctor looked at the sheriff, who nodded for him to continue. He then glanced at his chart for a moment and closed it. "Mrs. McCallister lost a lot of blood, and the blow to her head was substantial. We ran some tests, but we won't know for sure what her condition is until she regains consciousness—if she ever does. I'm sorry. I wish I had better news."

Smith put his arm around Abby, who leaned against him. At that moment, his phone buzzed with a text message. The medical examiner had bagged up The Don to take to the morgue.

Ritchie, being the reporter he was (or at least now wanted to be), felt the need to ask a follow-up question. "In your experience, doctor, could a person return to normal after sustaining injuries like the ones Madison

McAllister did?"

"It's hard to say. I'm sorry, I wish I had a better answer for you," the doctor answered.

Abby didn't know how she should react. It was her *mom*, but deep down she wasn't sure how she felt. Everyone was staring at her, waiting for her to say something, but she couldn't think of anything to say that didn't sound forced or fake, so she said, "Is it possible my mom could become a better person because of what happened to her?"

The doctor stared at Abby for a moment and smiled before answering, "I've seen stranger things happen."

CHAPTER 55

"SLOW DOWN. WHAT HAPPENED?" RITCHIE SAID as Julie hastily tried to explain what she had just witnessed. Abby and the Sheriff stood around the phone while Ritchie switched to speaker mode.

Julie more calmly told them the series of events that took place in La Jolla to which she was witness—the discovery of the illegal test facility hidden in an abandoned hospital, the recovery of several of the homeless people who were reported missing, the connection between Ron and the experiment. Julie left out the part about Thomas beating Ron to death, just in case the sheriff wanted to take legal action against him.

"Julie, is my dad okay?" Abby hesitantly asked.

"He's fine."

"What about Alex?"

"I'll let your dad tell you about it."

"He's there?"

"No. Stay where you are. Your father is on his way to the hospital and ambulances are transferring the rest of the homeless people they found in the facility. What about Don and your mom?"

Ritchie quickly replied, "It's not good. I'll tell you when I see you."

"Ritchie, stay there and learn everything you can. I'll stay here."

"Okay, boss," Ritchie said and hung up. "Abby, this probably isn't the ideal time to learn the ropes of reporting, but there will also never be a story like this one. You in?"

"I'm in."

"Let's go wait for your dad to arrive and hear his version of the events. This should be interesting."

"I can interview my brother, if he's up to it."

"I like the way you think. But let's not forget we have the sheriff here with us right now."

Abby jumped at the opportunity. "You're right, Ritchie. Uh, Sheriff Smith, what is your connection to the series of events that involved Ron and Don McCallister?"

"No comment," was his reply with a wink.

"Get used to it," Ritchie said as they walked down the sterile hallway of the hospital, leaving the sheriff standing alone.

CHAPTER 56

THE DISGRACED DOCTOR AND THE TWO YOUNG men who had been tasked with watching the test patients had fled the facility when they saw what had happened out front with Shaggy. They had made their way down to La Jolla Cove and were now hiding in one of the caves exposed only during a low tide. They had stopped at the corner liquor store to buy a bottle of rum to help them plan their escape. The unlikely trio sat there speechless and clueless as they passed the bottle back and forth until the doctor spoke first.

"Zihuatanejo," was all he said.

"What?"

"Zihuatanejo," the doctor repeated.

"What are you talking about?"

"That's where I'm going," he said and took a swig of the brown booze.

"Where is that, Mexico?"

"Haven't any of you seen the movie, *Shawshank Redemption*? Seriously. It's where Andy Dufresne goes after he escapes from prison and his pal Red follows later."

"That's a real place?"

"Yes, it's a real place."

"Is it near the ocean?"

"It's *on* the ocean."

"Good. If I have to leave La Jolla, I want to go somewhere warm with water."

"I said *I'm* going there. You two are on your own."

"Now wait a minute, Doc. I think we'd be better off if we stick together."

"How much money do you two have?"

"On us?"

"No, in your mutual funds. Yes, on you."

The pair pulled out their wallets and counted out forty-two dollars and eighteen cents.

"How much do you have, Doc?" The doctor realized that if he told the two he had $300 they would simply overpower him and steal his money, so he said he had about the same, forty bucks.

"We're gonna need more than $80 to escape," the doc said. "Anyone got any ideas?"

"What about that liquor store we were just at," one guy suggested. They do a good business. I say we rob them."

"Now we're armed robbers?" the doctor asked.

"No, we're murderers *and* armed robbers. You got a better idea, Doc?

"I guess not, but you two are the ones going in and I'll stand lookout."

"Fine, let's do it."

"Now?" the doc asked.

"Yes, I think they close in an hour."

The doctor took another long swig from the bottle. "Okay, let's roll."

The three men made their way out of the cave and

climbed the steep stairs to Prospect Avenue, fueled by desperation and the liquid courage the alcohol provided. The one thing they didn't have was a real plan—except for the doctor, who was planning to run the minute the other two went inside the store.

CHAPTER 57

"OH MY GOD—ALEX, ARE YOU OKAY?" THOMAS said when he opened the door to Ron's van and found his young son in the back with duct tape over his mouth and his hands bound behind his back.

Alex nodded while Thomas set Shaggy gently down in the passenger's seat.

"Alex, it's going to be okay," Thomas said with tears in his eyes. "This may hurt a little, but I'm going to remove the tape from your mouth on the count of three, okay?"

Again, Alex nodded.

"One, two—" and Thomas ripped the tape off before he got to three.

"What are you doing here, Dad?"

"Saving you, son."

"You said you were going to pull the tape off on three." Thomas smiled. Though he'd been estranged from Alex for a while, his son's humor was the same. And that he could even joke right now was a good sign.

"I couldn't wait to talk to you," Thomas said.

"Dad, Ron is not a nice person."

"Believe me, I know."

"Dad?"

"Yes, son."

"Are you going to take the tape off my hands?"

"Of course, sorry." Thomas hurried to finish freeing Alex. "I'm just so glad you're okay."

"Thanks for finding me, Dad. I've really missed you."

"I've missed you too. More than you know," Thomas said as he ran his hands through Alex's hair.

"Abby tells me all the time."

"She does? Good. That's good. Alex, now, I have to save my friend and get him to the hospital. Do you know if Ron left the keys to this van somewhere?"

"I don't know, Dad. Where's Abby?"

"She's okay, don't worry. I'll take you to her when I find the keys. Stay here with my friend Shaggy and I'll be right back."

"What about Ron? He could come back."

"Not a chance, I made sure of that."

"Good. I hope you taught him a lesson about the Golden Rule. You know, treat others how you want to be treated."

"Don't worry, Alex, I schooled him about being a bully and treated him just like he treated others… badly."

CHAPTER 58

"OPEN THE REGISTER AND GIVE US ALL THE money!" one of the would-be robbers yelled, trying to sound serious and intimidating at the same time.

The Asian woman behind the counter stared at him for a few seconds and then opened the cash drawer and started pulling out the money with one hand while she pushed the panic button with the other. It was designed to send a signal to the police, but her son had reprogrammed it to alert whomever was in the back room—and someone was always in the back room. She took her sweet time getting the money out knowing what was coming next. She put the cash in a bag to make sure it was easy to put back when this was all over.

"Come on, we don't have all day, lady."

"You said, 'we.' You are not alone?"

"No, my buddy is over there grabbing a few bottles of your best booze. I hope you don't mind."

She looked in the overhead mirror and saw someone pulling bottles off the shelf and smiled to herself. The family had a plan for two perpetrators. "I don't want any trouble," she said. "Does your friend need a bag?"

"Seriously?"

"Seriously," she answered nicely and casually.

"Uh, sure. Why not?"

"Tell him to bring what he wants up to the counter."

The man turned to tell his friend to bring the bounty up to the front, and when he did, the cashier calmly shot him twice in the back. Two seconds later, her husband appeared from the back room and shot the other one three times. Without a word, they each put a gun in the hand of the man the other had "shot," knowing the firearms would come back clean when run through a ballistics test. The panic button killed the camera, so there was no footage of what had happened. They would later explain it as a computer glitch when the authorities arrived and investigated the botched robbery attempt. After waiting a few more minutes to ensure the two men were dead, she dialed 911 and carefully put the money back in the cash drawer.

CHAPTER 59

THOMAS, ABBY, ALEX, JULIE, RITCHIE, AND Sheriff Smith pushed two tables together in the hospital cafeteria so they could talk about what had just transpired.

"Dad, what's going to happen to us?" Alex asked.

"Well, your mom is suddenly a very rich woman, so when she gets better you'll likely live with her."

"But we want to live with you."

"That would be great, buddy, but unlike your mom, I don't have any money… or a house."

The sheriff decided to spill what he knew about his recently departed friend. "Since this is going to come out anyway, there is something you should know, Thomas. When Don married Madison, he had her sign a prenuptial agreement, which pays her a quarter-million-dollar cash settlement in the event of his death or a divorce… whichever came first. She was constantly badgering him to change it after they were together a year, but Don still loved his first wife and left everything to her. He did have a life insurance policy that will pay Madison a half-million dollars. But my guess is, she'll need all that money and then some to pay for her long-term care."

Thomas was surprised. Madison had taken him for

everything he had, so why had she gone soft when it came to The Don, who was worth tens of millions of dollars. "Are you sure about the financial arrangement?" he asked the sheriff.

"All I know is what he told me. I don't think he fully trusted Madison, so he was careful. You don't get to be where he is, I mean *was*, without being a shrewd businessman."

Julie spoke up after thinking through what the sheriff had just said. "Thomas, you and the kids can stay with me on my boat."

"Thank you, I really appreciate the offer. Sheriff, with all that's happened, do you think the authorities would still enforce the order of protection my ex-wife took out against me?"

"I'll make some calls, but you are their father and as far as I can tell, they're lucky to have you in their lives."

"In that case," Thomas said, "what do you two say to living with me in my van?"

"Whoa! That doesn't sound like such a good idea," the sheriff said. "People are going to question that, and the authorities will have a hard time ignoring it."

"Well… right now, my van's parked inside my friend's garage, if that makes a difference."

"Which friend?" the sheriff asked.

"Max Webster. We played together on the Chargers."

"Oh, yeah. Of course I know who Max Webster is," the sheriff said. "You two were the best offensive linemen the team ever had."

"Plus, he's a great guy who lives alone in a big house not too far from here. Me and the kids would be in great hands there until we can sort things out."

"What will you do for money?" Julie asked Thomas.

"I honestly don't know," he answered.

"Dad, now that you're all cleaned up, maybe you could become a broadcaster!" Alex said excitedly. "Or a coach. You're a hero now!"

"Those are great ideas, son. I'll think about it. But the truth is, your sister is the real hero and you're a very brave boy."

"I could get a job to help with money," Alex offered.

"Thanks, son, but hopefully that won't be necessary."

"Well," Abby announced, "no matter what, I'm going to become a writer."

"You're hired," Julie quickly replied. And she meant it.

EPILOGUE

WHERE ARE THEY NOW?
By Abby MacDonald, Reporter
Beach and Bay News

It's been over a year since I started writing this column, and for the past few months, many of you have contacted me wanting to know what happened to everyone entangled in the scandal involving my famous father and the people who lived in the homeless camp on the point. Much of what happened is chronicled in the best-selling novel, The Homeless Hero *by Ritchie Goldman, the reporter who wrote this column before handing it off to me.*

So I'll begin with an update on him, my mentor. He's now a reporter for the San Diego Union-Tribune and married to his long-suffering girlfriend (his words). His book has been optioned for a feature film—he's hard at work on a screenplay. (He hasn't told me who will play the part of Abby in the film, but I'm lobbying for Kiernan Shipka from television's Mad Men.*)*

My father, Thomas MacDonald, the former All-Pro lineman for the San Diego Chargers and the true homeless hero, is still living in his van—only it's parked in front of the new house he is building for our family. (Many of the people he played with and against got together and held a fundraiser so my father could build us a brand-new home.) He quit drinking and is in the best shape of his life. My dad is even being honored by the NFL as the first retired player to receive the Walter Payton Man-of-the-Year Award at this year's Pro Bowl game in Hawaii—and my brother and I are going with him.

Too many of the homeless people who were used for human testing did not survive their ordeal. Their names are listed at the end of this article. One of the few who did pull through was my father's best friend, Ron "Shaggy" Washington. He's back to full strength and living with many of the others who were displaced by the development at Mariner's Beach Park. The City of San Diego broke ground on the new complex for the homeless before building the commercial elements of the plan called McCallister Park. The hotel for the homeless (unofficially called "The Don") was fast-tracked and offers housing for individuals and families who would have otherwise been on the street. The people from the park are allowed to live there rent free for as long as they like as part of the settlement with the City—my father passed on the offer. He did ask for and received a monument to be erected in honor of the late Jeff Wiener, a tireless advocate for the homeless.

My mom, Madison MacDonald, passed away peacefully a few months ago after never regaining consciousness from her injuries. My brother and I forgave her for what she did and miss her. We used most of the money from the sale of our old house and our inheritance to start a fund to help homeless families. I plan to become a journalism major when I graduate from high school, and my brother wants to become a football player like our father. We have saved enough money to pay for our tuition—although Alex believes he will get a full-ride football scholarship. My dad coaches his flag football team and says my brother will be better than him someday.

Sheriff Bob Smith was investigated and cleared of any wrongdoing and was reelected for another term. (He ran unopposed, so we knew he would win.) In his free time, he searched for the disgraced doctor who escaped justice for his role in the illegal testing on the homeless. After months of searching, he found the doctor in a small fishing village in Baja named Trancones and brought him back to face charges.

There were never any charges filed against anyone for the beating death of Ron McCallister. The claims made against my father's friends who conducted a citizen's arrest of Ron's accomplices were deemed baseless, so they were cleared of any wrongdoing and, in fact, received an award from the City for their heroism.

My editor insisted I leave her out of this article, but Julie has become more than a boss. She's like a mother to me. I don't know what I would have done without her. We're best friends, and she and my dad started dating a few months ago… and I've never seen him happier.

MAIN CAST OF CHARACTERS

Thomas "Big Mac" MacDonald, homeless former pro football player

Abby MacDonald, Thomas's daughter, age 12

Alex MacDonald, Thomas's son, age 9

Ritchie Goldman, columnist and reporter for the *Beach and Bay News*

Julie Best, editor and publisher of the *Beach and Bay News*

Don "The Don" McCallister, real estate developer

Mrs. Madison MacDonald-McCallister, Thomas's former wife and Don's current wife

Ron McCallister, son of Don McCallister (leader, Bird Rock Band of Brothers)

Ron "Shaggy" Washington, Thomas's homeless friend

Mike "Teen Wolf" Sandoval, Thomas's homeless friend, lawyer, and gambler

Jeffrey Wiener, homeless advocate

Les Davis, marina dockmaster

Bob "Smitty" Smith, San Diego County Sheriff and longtime friend of Don McCallister

Jack "Bullet" Moniker, bartender and former cop

who took a bullet for his partner

Suzy, staffer for San Diego City Councilman

Red, Smokey Joe, and Shooter, Thomas's homeless friends and war veterans

Max Webster, Thomas's friend and former teammate

AUTHOR NOTES

Where to start? I know what you're thinking, start at the beginning. Nah, too obvious. Let's jump around. First of all, I wish all authors would put "liner notes" in their books to explain what they were thinking when they wrote their book—except Stephen King, I don't think I want to know what was going on in his head. As an avid reader, I would like to learn (after I have read the book) who the author based certain characters on and what places inspired certain scenes—so here are my author confessions (in no particular order).

The opening scene with my main character buried and breathing through a straw was the very first thing I thought of for this book. I just didn't know how it tied in to the rest of the story because I didn't have a story at that point—which, for the record, was in 2010, long before Carl Hiaasen's book *Kink No Surrender* hit the shelves in 2014. That book has a somewhat similar scene, which horrified me when I read it. Then I realized, "Hey, one of my favorite authors had the same idea I did. Too cool." I don't know if Carl Hiaasen did this or not, but I considered digging a ditch and burying myself to see what it would feel like, but I worried that could be how *my* story would end. So instead, I had my kids cover me with sand at the beach while I wheezed through a Starbucks straw. It was awful. Speaking of awful....

I lived on the streets to experience homelessness for several days. To prepare, I let myself go and added on a ton of weight (so I wouldn't starve or freeze... yes, San Diego nights can get cold). Of course, those things weren't going to happen, so the truth was, I really just wanted to eat whatever I wanted for a while... and not have to shave. I wouldn't say I had a Duck Dynasty beard, but it wasn't pretty. In fact, my wife threw me out of the house a day before I was planning to leave because I was already a filthy mess.

The plan was to live on the beach for a week with only forty bucks in my pocket and what I could carry on my back. I figured with McDonald's Dollar Menu I could make it through the week even if I didn't earn a dime. But my idea was to collect recycling and turn it in for cash, which I did when I ran out of money... after less than two days. No, I didn't blow the money on booze. Instead, I befriended other homeless people and would buy them lunch or coffee so we could sit (safely) while they told me their story. It was so worth the money, too.

Although most of what I learned didn't make it in the book, I found it fascinating and enlightening all the same. For example, some of the most informed people don't have a home or a job—which allows them to catch up on their reading. Many of those I met on the streets read the daily paper from front to back (assuming they could find one with all the sections intact).

I also learned that a few poor choices combined with

a little bad luck could be the difference between living in a car and having a home. As I sat and listened to one sad story after another, I realized how easy it could have been for me to be the one begging for buck on a street corner rather than begging you to buy my book. Sure, many of the people panhandling could be doing it to make a fast buck, but I found as I tried my hand at the art of asking others for money it's not for the faint of heart. I made a sign that read, "I dare you to hit me with a quarter," and I was pelted with money. The idea was not an original one, but it worked. I made enough in two hours to eat like a king (at Burger King) and buy meals for others I met on the streets—much to the chagrin of management.

If you live in San Diego (or have visited here more than once), you may recognize some of the locations. That was by design. I grew up surfing at Big Rock Beach in La Jolla and the secret scenic lookouts are real (my friends and I spent days looking for Munchkinville, too), so there is authenticity to the locals. That said, I blended places together to form a hybrid of fictional spots (Mariner's Beach Park being one of them) that had a ring of truth but were clearly not real. I hope that doesn't throw off anyone trying to find the actual places I put in the book. It's factual fiction.

Speaking of factual fiction, if you read this book and wondered, Is he talking about so-and-so? let it go. I simply made the characters up. And if I didn't, I would never write and tell. Could Big Mac be…? The answer is no. He's not real. I did name him after John D. MacDonald, my favorite author, but that's the only connection to someone living or dead—mostly dead. There is no Shaggy or Wiener or Smokey Joe, but man, would they be interesting people to hang out with.

One person who indirectly influenced this book is the late Gary Taylor. I often surf at a place called Swami's in Encinitas—at least once a week—and as I walk down to the break, I always pass the memorial to Gary. He was a recognized writer for a community newspaper based in North County San Diego, as well as a Swami's local and a great guy who died way too young. I'm fortunate that we had forged a friendship around surfing and writing, and he went out of his way to support my surf shops and my books. He was a friend, a surfing companion, and an equal when it came to writing. Because of Gary, I hold community newspapers in the highest regard. In the book I downplay their significance (and Ritchie's role in them), but the truth is, I think they are the most important media for people who live in urban (and even rural) areas.

Haters. I was so thrilled by the sales and success of my first novel. It really resonated with readers and took off in way that inspired me to write another novel—the one you are reading. However, some of the haters who posted nasty reviews almost ruined me. The common complaint was the editing wasn't complete. So, for this book, I asked a circle of reviewers to read my manuscript and correct it, paying them a fee for every mistake they uncovered. It was well it worth it. Two readers in particular (Janet Williams and Mary Valerio) were quick to catch mistakes. Others offered valuable feedback. This is one time where being wrong is right (for me, anyway).

In additional to editorial reviewers, I sent the early versions of this book to tweens and parents of tweens to make sure that Abby was neither immature nor too mature for her twelve years. The responses were all over the board. I left a lot in the book that some parents loved and others loathed. But the thing I focused on was to make sure this book was okay for kids aged 10 and above. That—according to the early reviewers—was accomplished. There is no profanity or promiscuous behavior. There are no "awkward" scenes.

Last, but not least, is the tradition that began with my first novel, *Runaway Best Seller*, I took pictures of the places in the book. That first book was set in Hawaii so I had to go back and photograph and post the photographs from the locales featured in the novel. For *The Homeless Hero* I simply had to ride my bike to take pictures of the places in this book. I created a Pinterest page of pictures of the places that inspired this story. I encourage you to take a peak at what inspired the stories and the story lines, as well as to see what's real and what's not, at www.pinterest.com/leesilber.

Last (but certainly not least), let me share something with you that you may or may not already know: We authors love to hear from readers. Now let me qualify that statement, there is n-o-t-h-i-n-g better than a reader reaching out to say they loved the book. It's what we writers live for—positive feedback. We authors are sensitive, insecure, and unsure about our work, so any validation that we "don't suck" is welcomed.

Aside from reviews on Amazon, your emailed opinions are greatly appreciated and you can reach me at leesilber@leesilber.com. Lastly, thank YOU for reading my book and making it all the way to the end. What? You skipped to this part first? Congratulations, you are a right-brainer (which means one of my business books would be perfect for you). Seriously, thanks for taking the time to read the book and these comments.

Lee Silber
Mission Beach, California

ACKNOWLEDGEMENTS

This book wouldn't exist if I hadn't stumbled onto *A Tan and Sandy Silence* by author John MacDonald back in 1978. It was the first mystery novel I'd ever read and I was hooked—at the age of thirteen (close to the same age Abby is in this book). I have since read every title in the Travis McGee series several times and owe Mr. MacDonald a deep debt of gratitude for opening my eyes to what works and what doesn't when it comes to writing in this genre. (You will notice I named my main character after my favorite author.)

Some of my earliest memories are of my mom taking me to the local library to check out books. Her love of reading was passed down to me, and our mutual respect and admiration for libraries (and librarians) is shared to this day. Many of my earlier books were researched and written in libraries around San Diego, especially the central library on E Street. The new main library is amazing, but I will strangely miss the old one for sentimental reasons.

In school I found some subjects extremely excruciating (math and science) and others I excelled at (art and writing). There were a couple of teachers who encouraged me to pursue what I enjoyed and did well and, for that, I thank them for changing the trajectory of my life. They assured me I was not dumb and to go where my strengths took me.

I am the son of a son of a salesman and, even though my father didn't necessarily understand what I wanted to do with my life, he supported me all the same. That's unconditional love. I have the same kind of love and support from my wife of twenty years. She has hung in there during the lean years when it looked like I would have to possibly get a real job and give up on my dream, but she believed in me when I didn't always believe in myself.

It's hard to make it as a writer, and it's impossible without the help of others. I thank my good friend, publishing entrepreneur Andrew Chapman, for being both a sounding board and offering sound advice about everything from dialogue to design. I am also indebted to my literary agent, Toni Lopopolo, for her contributions to my career. I wish I could list everyone—from my friends who are willing to read and critique my early drafts, to my band who play at all my book-related events, to the readers of my earlier works who are willing to write reviews that keep me wanting to stay up late and finish these books.

For *The Homeless Hero* I decided to hold a "find the flaws" contest and paid people based on the number of typos they found. Needless to say, there were plenty. Here are the readers who reveled in the role of grammarian—Anthony Delellis, Stephanie Diehl, Ellen Goodwin, Susan Fall, Gail Morgan, Gordon Rhodes, Rita Rule, Mary Valerio, and Janet Williams. Many thanks to all of them. If you find something they missed (don't blame them, please), let me know and I will mention you in the updated version—after I fix what you found. Contact me at leesilber@leesilber.com.

Last, but certainly not least, I thank my two young sons, Ethan and Evan. You both inspire me to want to be the best person (and best writer) I can possibly be. I do it all for you.

ABOUT THE AUTHOR

Before becoming the best-selling author of 20 books, Lee Silber lived an interesting life. He was a surf shop owner, pen salesman, graphic artist, corporate trainer, keynote speaker, and marketing consultant. What he had was success in a number of areas; what he lacked, gratefully, was ever hitting rock bottom. So, to write *The Homeless Hero,* Silber knew he needed to discover what it was truly like to live on the streets—and that he did. It was both terrifying and enlightening at the same time. He survived, however, and currently lives comfortably with his wife and two young sons in Mission Beach, California. To read more about how Lee lived on the streets to research this book and how he is now giving back to help the homeless, go to www.LeeSilber.com.

Made in the USA
Columbia, SC
10 July 2022